JESS MOWRY

GHOST TRAIN

HENRY HOLT AND COMPANY
NEW YORK

Henry Holt and Company, Inc.
Publishers since 1866
115 West 18th Street
New York, New York 10011

Henry Holt is a registered
trademark of Henry Holt and Company, Inc.

Published in Canada by Fitzhenry & Whiteside Ltd.,
195 Allstate Parkway, Markham, Ontario L3R 4T8.

Library of Congress Cataloging-in-Publication Data
Mowry, Jess. Ghost train / by Jess Mowry.
p.   cm
Summary: Thirteen-year-old Remi, who has just moved
to California from Haiti, and his neighbor Niya travel back in time
to solve the mystery of the night train.
[1. Supernatural—Fiction. 2. Time travel—Fiction. 3. Haitian Americans—Fiction.
4. Afro-Americans—Fiction.] I. Title.
PZ7.M86655Gh   1996   [Fic]—dc20   96-10291

ISBN 0-8050-4440-X
First Edition—1996

Printed in the United States of America on acid-free paper. ∞

1   3   5   7   9   10   8   6   4   2

To Apollo
Special thanks to Wayne French

GHOST TRAIN

The sound of the train woke him . . . rhythmic panting puffs like the breath of some huge jungle beast. It was coming slowly, creeping closer, the click and clack of its wheels echoing over the clang of its signal bell. The sounds were familiar to Remi, but also strange, as so many things in this new land were; familiar enough to comfort a little yet strange enough to remind him that he was an outsider here.

He sat up in bed, feeling the oncoming rumble of iron deep in his bones like the booming bass beat of a funeral march. Outside it was night, and long past twelve o'clock, yet his room was lit daylight bright by glaring electric rays. He peered through the grimy-glassed window and seemingly straight into the engine's blazing eye, even from here in his second-floor room.

He pushed off his blankets and crouched naked on the narrow bed, pressing his nose to cold glass. The locomotive neared, gigantic and black.

American trains were so big, Remi thought; probably sized in proportion to cross this vast land. And yet he could see that this huge machine was only a switchyard engine. Pale steam puffed from in front of its wheels, swirling in shapes made ghostly by the ice-blue tinge of its head-lamp arc. The blood-red flare from its firebox flickered beneath the cab, reflecting off rails polished bright by its passing. Remi's window wouldn't open. It was sealed shut by what could have been a century of paint—yet the scents of oil smoke and hot steel burned strong in his nostrils, while streamers of steam rose up to surround him with shivery dampness. The ancient house shook as the engine came closer, chuffing and clanging, until he could feel the fierce heat of its headlamp beating his face.

He drew back: the oncoming engine seemed somehow aware of him at the window. And it seemed to be heading straight into the house. He wanted to run, but he couldn't move. He crouched there, frozen, braced for the crash, but then came a shrieking of steel upon steel as the train took a curve in the tracks and puffed slowly past. Remi looked down, his fear fading now, replaced by an urge to wave to the driver as any boy might. But he saw only a shadow in the cab, backlit by the boiler's flame-glow. Again he felt fingers of steam clammy and wet on his skin. The engine passed, its pistons hissing and scraping, and its bell still clanging a sad-sounding note. A line of low flatcars followed, rocking and swaying and rumbling over the rails. They were loaded with long sheets of steel, big iron beams, and shapes of massive machinery. One carried a huge ship's propeller, and two men sat on the edge of a blade. It was too dark for Remi to see them clearly, but one man seemed to reach into his pocket before facing the other, maybe to offer a cigarette. Then the car passed from Remi's sight. More followed. He watched, still feeling the old house tremble and shake beneath him. The train was entering what looked like a shipyard. A vista of glaring arc-lamps, great looming shapes, and skeletal crane booms spread out under velvet-black sky. Remi thought he could see a big ship taking form almost before his eyes. There had been similar scenes in Port-au-Prince, Haiti, where he'd been born, of fire and smoke and steel and steam. They were familiar even here, in Oakland, California, in the United States of America. Familiar yet strange, like the night train itself. There was a whole new world to learn about here, and one day and part of a night had only given him hints.

Then his sight seemed to blur as if rain had flooded the window. He rubbed his eyes. The shipyard seemed to shimmer and fade like a dream. He yawned. Maybe soot from the engine had covered the glass? He was tired. There was a three-hour time difference between here and Haiti, as his father had explained, and this seemed to further confuse him and add to the strangeness of things in the night. He lay back down on his unfamiliar bed, drawing the blankets around him once more, and drifted into a sleep that was troubled by the clanging of bells and the clanking of iron.

He woke hours later to find weak gray fog light filtering through window glass steamed by his breath. It was early morning on what would be his first day of school in this new land. He didn't know the time, though his mother had said she would buy him a clock for his bedside. His very own clock.

He rolled from the bed. The morning air was

chill—another new strangeness—yet he paused a moment before dressing to look around. His very own room! True, it was small: four bare walls with lath peeking in places where plaster had fallen, and a scarred hardwood floor that hadn't been varnished for decades, but all his own with a door he could close to be alone. On the door was a mirror, cloudy and dim, yet also his own. He saw himself now, an *American* boy of thirteen. His body was slender, and black as midnight, with a gently framed build that gave him more tummy than chest. Obsidian eyes looked back from a narrow-jawed face, and big white teeth smiled from behind proud lips. His hair was bushy and thick, yet to be cut in a U.S.A. style like those he'd seen in American movies or on Afro-American tourists around Port-au-Prince. His clothes would pass for the time being: blue denim shorts, well-worn Nikes, and a cherished white tank top a little too large with a Rastafarian lion on its front. This shirt had drawn some disapproving stares in parts of Port-au-Prince from wealthy people and soldiers, but there would be no problem here because American people could wear whatever they wished and not be afraid of offending the government. Remi dressed, then studied himself in the mirror once more. Around his neck on a slim strip of leather hung a small cross carved of ironwood. It was smooth and polished from his skin, and hardly a shade lighter. Then he remembered the train and glanced toward the window, but everything outside was shrouded by fog.

"Remi!" his mother's voice called.

"Coming!"

The door to his room opened into the kitchen, where his mother stood at the stove preparing an American breakfast of bacon and eggs and toast. She was a fine-boned woman with a hint of gold in her eyes and full lips always ready to smile. Remi glanced around the little kitchen. He had no illusions about this house—it was ancient and showing its age and stood in the poorer part of the city down by the waterfront wharves. Yet his mother and father and he had the whole second floor to themselves. True, the stove was old, but it was a *real* stove with an oven and not just an iron gas ring. And there was a refrigerator, made by General Electric. And the kitchen sink had *two* faucets, one of which supplied *hot* water in moments. This was also true of the sink in the bathroom, and for once in his life Remi didn't need to be told to go wash before breakfast.

His father was at the table when Remi returned. A tall slender man, he was dressed today in his best suit of clothes, his ebony face a handsome contrast to his spotless white shirt and blue necktie. Some dishes and silverware had been left by the former tenants, along with most of the furniture. Everything was old and shabby but still good enough to begin a new life. Remi's father sipped coffee from a chipped crockery mug and smiled. "Did you sleep well, my son?"

Remi sat down and took a mug of coffee his mother handed him. "Yes. Except for the train in the night."

His parents exchanged glances, then shrugged. "We did not hear a train," said his father. "But we were very tired, and you have younger ears."

Remi started on his bacon and eggs, discovering how hungry he was. "Well, this train could have woken the dead."

His mother frowned slightly and ruffled his hair. "Do not say such things. Perhaps it was only a dream. Hurry now, and do not be late for school. You have the directions?"

Remi patted the pocket of his shorts, feeling the folded paper inside. "Yes. And maybe I will meet other students on the way."

His mother glanced to the fog-clouded kitchen window. "It is cold outside, and you are not used to it. After school we will shop for a jacket." She regarded Remi for a moment. "And why are you wearing that shirt? It is next to nothing."

"It is my best."

"It is *not* your best. Your best is white and has buttons. American boys do not run about half-naked."

Remi made a face. "American boys do not wear white shirts that button! *This* is most like what they wear. And I will have the *right* kind of jacket."

His mother nodded. "For warmth."

But his father smiled. "I do not think warmth is his first consideration. Style seems more important to American boys."

"It will be warm, no matter what his consideration," his mother said firmly.

A few minutes later Remi stepped out into the hall and closed the apartment's door behind him. It had three heavy locks that used separate keys, and the landlady, a sour-faced old woman, had warned that all should be bolted both night and day. After locking them carefully, Remi walked down the hall and descended the staircase to the ground floor. The entrance door was also fitted with formidable locks, and there were bars on its small colored-glass window. But these things were familiar sights, and many fine houses in Haiti had wrought-iron grilles on their windows and doors. This house had probably been grand in its day: a three-story structure of wood in Victorian style. There were signs that it had been many colors beneath its faded and peeling white paint. But now the front porch was rotten and sagging, and weeds filled the narrow front yard. The fog was still thick on the street, but Remi could make out the roofs and top floors of other buildings nearby. He passed through the gate in the ramshackle fence and out onto the sidewalk. He paused a moment, then turned right, curious to see how close the railroad tracks ran. The noise from trains may have had something to do with the apartment's rent being so reasonable.

"Yo!"

Remi stopped and turned around. A girl about his own age had come out of the house. She was dressed, American style, in big baggy jeans, zebra-striped Cons, and an oversized purple sweatshirt. Remi recognized the cartoon character on the front of the shirt as Taz the Tasmanian Devil, even though he wore braids and a backward-turned cap. The girl's skin was a beautiful dark chocolate tone. Her round-cheeked face was framed by tight-woven braids a lot longer and neater than Taz's and brightened by colored beads. Her nose was wide and small-bridged, and her full lips posed in a perpetual pout that seemed both sly and shy. She locked the door behind her, then skipped down the steps. As she neared, Remi saw that her eyes were a rich tawny-brown.

"You the G from upstairs?" she asked.

Remi knew what "G" meant from the rap songs blasted by boom boxes on Port-au-Prince streets, though he'd never been called one before. He supposed it was sort of a compliment here. "Um, yes. My name is Remi DuMont."

The girl's eyes seemed amused, but also showed interest. "I'm Niya Bedford. Me an' my mom live on the ground floor."

Remi bowed slightly. "I am happy to meet you, Mademoiselle Bedford."

The girl studied Remi and giggled. "Yo. You a French brutha or somethin'?"

"I am from Haiti. We do speak French there, but not the same dialect as spoken in France."

"Sounds more like French-fried Rastafarian."

Remi smiled. "Reggae music is popular in Haiti. Also American hip-hop. I am down with it."

"Yeah? Me, too. Are you boat people, like they talk about on TV?"

"No . . . though we left Haiti for many of the same reasons. We were not the poorest of poor. At least, not always."

Niya studied him again. "You don't look like you starvin'."

Remi pulled in his tummy a little. "My father's income was enough to keep food on our table. But there are many ways to be hungry."

Niya looked thoughtful. "My mom said somethin' like that once. So, what's your dad gonna do here?"

"He is going to work at the university in Berkeley, as a consultant on Haitian culture. He taught at a school in Port-au-Prince, but there are many . . . changing winds in our system. What is in favor today may put you in prison tomorrow."

"So, what grade you in, Remi?"

"The eighth."

Niya giggled again. "Yeah? So am I, but you already sound like you graduated from college."

Remi smiled once more. "My father also taught English."

"Yeah? Well, that sure ain't the 'English' you hear around this hood! Yo, maybe we'll have some classes together. You any good at math?"

"Well, it is not one of my favorite subjects."

"Me neither. But I'm takin' French, too. Parley view franchise."

". . . Oh. Well, that is . . . not exactly like the French you hear around Haiti."

Niya glanced at her watch, a plastic digital in shocking pink. "So, c'mon, Remi. Or we gonna be late."

The fog was thinning as Remi walked up the street at Niya's side. The neighborhood, he saw, was as shabby as the house. There were many old buildings of crumbling brick and rusty sheet metal. Some were boarded, others just blackened and burnt-out shells. Those still in use seemed mostly small shops that repaired trucks and other machinery. All had bars on their windows and doors, and all were covered in layers of spray-painted symbols and words. The neighborhood was very dirty, and that was something else familiar yet strange because a lot of what had been thrown away would have been put to instant use in Haiti. In front of one shop stood a huge ship's propeller, about eight feet across from blade to blade tip. Remi recalled the one he had seen on the night train.

"Niya? Do trains pass the house every night?"

Niya shrugged. "Well, there's a bunch of tracks about two blocks down by the docks. Sometimes you can hear trains pretty loud, when the wind blows in off the bay. You get used to it."

Remi glanced back down the street, still mostly hidden in mist. "It will take me some time to get used to what happened last night. But I suppose that is why the rent is so low."

Niya turned to Remi, and her eyes, like her lips, now seemed both sly and shy. Then she grinned, looking boyish. "Nah. The rent's cheap 'cause the house is haunted!"

2

I never had nobody carry my books before. It's kinda cool."

It was mid-afternoon, with the sun bright and hot, a different sort of heat from what Remi was used to—drier, and so more comfortable. He had noted that his shorts and tank top fit in with the other kids' clothes, and throughout the school day no one had paid much attention to him unless he opened his mouth. School itself had been yet another strange but familiar experience, though he'd been surprised to find that much of what was being taught here to eighth graders was what he had already learned in fourth. The math teacher had talked about "bumping" him up to high school, but he wasn't sure he cared for that idea—not after finding that he and Niya shared many classes. He'd been amazed at having to pass through a metal detector in the school building entrance, and then annoyed by being forced to submit to a full-body search by a guard before he could enter the office to pick up his schedule. He had seen several senseless fights in the halls, while an entire class was devoted to nothing but drug, gang, and sexual awareness. He would have said "wasted" because most of the kids either seemed to know more about those subjects than the teacher, or just didn't care. Of course, even in Haiti there had been talk of the violence and drugs in America, and yet Remi couldn't help wondering *why* so many of these kids were fighting with one another. They had so *much!* Even the poorest-dressed boy he'd seen would have looked like a hip-hop fashion model among the street children of Port-au-Prince. Most seemed to be well-fed; in fact, some were astonishingly fat, and certainly none were starving. The school lunch had been huge, and Remi recalled many times in his life having had less food to eat in a day. From talk overheard, he'd learned that everyone owned a TV, a luxury his parents had never been able to afford even in the best of times.

There were a million things he wanted to ask Niya about this new place, but something he *did* seem to have that most American kids didn't was patience. Just walking in the afternoon sun with her was everything he needed for the moment. Besides, it gave him time to try and digest all the experiences he'd had that day. His head, like his stomach, was almost too full, and he'd picked up a lot of new phrases and words. Most of them were definitely not the "English" he'd been taught, and Niya often giggled when he tried them out on her.

"Um, this 'capping'? I have heard it in songs, but I am not really sure what it means."

Niya looked sad. "Killin' somebody, what it mean." She sighed and counted on her delicate fingers. "Also, wastin', icin', kickin', an' givin' some sucka a dirt nap."

"Oh." Remi pulled on one strap of his tank top that had slipped off his shoulder. "So many 'cool' words for death. But death is never cool."

"Got that right," Niya murmured.

Remi found himself sorry he'd asked, but then smiled, hoping to cheer Niya. "Dirt nap. That sounds like something a zombie would do."

Niya's face turned thoughtful. "Well, there's a lotta people in the hood ain't much more'n zombies—crackheads an' winos an' dope-smokin' fools." She smiled, too, and then reached shyly to pull up Remi's other strap. "You got voodoo in Haiti, huh?"

"*Voodun*. But it is not what you see in American horror films. *Voodun* is a respected form of religion in many parts of the world, and has little to do with sticking pins into dolls. My father is something of an expert on the subject, and of other things that some would call supernatural. It is one of the reasons he is now working at the university."

Niya pointed. "But you're wearin' a cross."

Remi shrugged. "I am a respecter of *Voodun*, but not a follower." He glanced at Niya, then added, "I have seen a few things in my time that American science might have trouble explaining." He puffed his small chest a little. "My father has often said that I may be sensitive to the supernatural."

Niya cocked her head. "Like seein' ghosts, what you sayin'?"

"Well, I have never actually *seen* one. But this"—Remi fingered the small wooden carving—"is more of a family heirloom. It was worn by an ancestor of mine, a slave who escaped to the forest and founded our family. It is said that he was sensitive, too. But to me this is not a religious symbol, only a reminder of how things used to be."

Niya nodded. "Yeah. I know what you sayin', Remi. I go to church with my mom every Sunday, but there gotta be more to God than singin' an' preachin' one day a week, so guess I ain't much of a believer, neither."

Remi smiled. "Not even in ghosts?"

"Huh?"

"This morning. When we met. You told me the house was haunted."

Niya giggled. "Oh, *that*. Well, the landlady won't talk about it, but the people who lived in our apartment before said somethin' to my mom when they was movin' out. Wack stuff goin' on in the basement." She turned to Remi, her expression more serious now. "Believe this, B, it's Spook Central down there. Only one little window an' a piddly light bulb. That's where the washer an' dryer is, an' I do the laundry, but only in the *daytime*. I wouldn't go down there at night if you stuck a gun in my ear!"

They had arrived at the house, and Remi gazed

up at the ancient three-story structure. "Well, it *is* very old. . . . By American standards, anyhow. And it is the sort of house often shown as haunted in horror movies." He cupped his chin in one hand and studied the house a few moments more, then turned to Niya. "There are houses far older in Haiti. And many of them are known to have what my father calls manifestations. But have you ever actually seen anything in the basement?"

"Well, no. It's more of a feelin' . . . a real creepy feelin'. Like something's watchin' . . . an' maybe *waitin'!*" Niya giggled. "Yo! If it's really a ghost, it's prob'ly a white one who's all pissed off about black people livin' in his house."

Remi regarded the old house again. To one side of the high front porch was a dusty little window at ground level. He gazed at the small square of darkness. "My mother will be using that washer and dryer soon. Maybe I should . . . check out this place. Are the stairs safe?"

Niya smiled slightly. "Ain't nuthin' safe in this hood, Remi. C'mon. We'll go peep it together. And . . . after . . . maybe we could work on our homework awhile? At my crib?"

"Cri—? . . . Oh." Remi smiled, too. "Yes, that

would be . . . kickin'. But my mother may want to take me shopping for a jacket. I must see her first." Then he heard a distant and almost familiar sound. He turned to stare down toward the waterfront. Two blocks away a train was slowly crossing the street. The engine was a red and black diesel. Smoke spouted from its stack, but it certainly wasn't chugging along spewing steam like the big fire-breathing beast he'd seen the night before. He noticed now that railroad tracks ran up the middle of the street and curved sharply into a field of dry weeds alongside the house. But the rails were red with rust, except where polished by the passing of truck and car tires.

"A moment, Niya." Remi balanced the stack of books on the gatepost and went down the sidewalk. Yes, the rails ran right under his window and into the trash-littered field, and they were rotted with rust and buried by weeds. The wooden ties beneath them were decayed soft as mush. Remi followed the tracks with his eyes. The line went on past the house toward what looked like a scrap yard. Two rusty crane booms thrust skyward along mountains of junk and wrecked cars. No big ship was being built there, or had been for a long, long time. A fence of weathered old boards topped with sagging barbed wire ran right across the abandoned rail line, and Remi could see no sign of a gate that a train could pass through.

He stood for a minute, a frown on his face, but then shrugged and came back up the sidewalk. His mother had been right: he'd just dreamed the night train. Maybe he'd heard the sounds of a real locomotive from down by the docks and it had invaded his mind as sounds sometimes do during dreams. After all, it was plain as day that no train had run on these rails in his lifetime.

Niya was waiting at the gate. "So, what were you lookin' for, Remi?"

Shrugging again, Remi took the books from the gatepost. "No matter. It is nothing." He followed Niya into the house and up the first-floor hallway to her door, standing near as she unlocked the locks and pushed it open.

"My mom won't be home till about eight," she said. "Maybe we could watch TV or somethin' after we do our homework?"

Remi glanced in, seeing a neatly kept living room with old but well cared-for furniture. He turned to Niya, suddenly wondering what she would look like in something besides those big baggy jeans and that shapeless T-shirt. "I will . . . check with my mother." He rolled his eyes. "She wants me to have a warm jacket."

Niya smiled, taking her books. "I'll be here. Aw river, Remi."

". . . Oh. *Au revoir*, Niya."

Remi dashed up the stairs two at a time, arriving at his own door panting, then wasted seconds sorting keys for the trio of locks before finally gaining entrance. To his amazement, a TV set now stood on a table in the living room. He stared, then approached it almost warily, wondering if this was another dream. It wasn't new, he saw—in a dream it surely would be—but it didn't look very old, either. It was a Philco, made in America, and a color model. He touched the blank face of the screen, then studied the control panel. The power cord wasn't plugged into the wall.

"Mother?"

His mother appeared in the kitchen doorway. Her smile seemed both shy and sly. "Yes?"

"Where did this come from?"

"The flea market. Though I would have called it the thieves' market. There is everything on earth for sale. Forty dollars for a color television was impossible to resist."

"But it might not work."

"Madame assured me it does. And your mother is not such a poor judge of character. I had hoped that my educated son might assemble it. There are . . . *lapin*—"

Remi grinned, seeing a set of antennae beside the TV. "*Rabbit* ears, Mom." He studied the connections. "This is a simple matter."

"But first I have another surprise for my American boy. Come."

Hardly daring to imagine new wonders, Remi followed his mother into his room. There on the bed lay not one but *two* jackets! He grabbed them both. "Mom! These are . . . *cool!*"

His mother shrugged. "I have seen the styles vain young men wear."

Remi gazed at the jackets, one in each hand. Both were used but in almost new condition. One was blue denim, bulky, with many pockets and zippers. He'd seen several like it that day, and had admired them. But the other . . .

"I . . . cannot wear this one."

His mother raised an eyebrow. "But why? I have seen other young men wearing them."

Remi lay the Raiders jacket aside. "It signifies a gang. To wear it is death."

His mother's eyes saddened. "Oh. Yes, I had almost forgotten. Even in America the young are not safe."

Remi nodded. "I have learned many things today, and one is that wearing a jacket like this can get you a dirt nap."

". . . Dirt . . . ?" His mother considered this for a moment, then frowned. "A childish expression for something so serious. But it seems just as childish for the young to fight among themselves when there is so much to share." She shook her head and sighed. "Is the other jacket safe to wear? And do you like it?"

"Oh, yes! It kicks!" Remi ran to his mother and kissed her. "Thank you!"

His mother smiled once again. "See that you also have a clock of your own, so there will be no excuses for losing track of time."

Remi examined the small digital clock his mother had placed on the windowsill above his bed. "Thank you! And now I will get our new TV goin' on!"

Attaching the antennae was a simple job, and it was obvious how to plug the power cord into the wall, even though the socket was different from those in Haiti. Just moments later the screen was alive with a commercial. Remi's mother sat down on the couch and frowned. "What is that slimy mess? It looks disgusting!"

"Oh. It is Gak. A boy at school had some."

"But . . . what does it *do?*"

". . . It . . . well . . . it is simply disgusting."

His mother sighed. "I suppose there are such things, though I wonder *why* there are such things. Come sit beside me and interpret awhile. Your English is far better than mine."

Remi hesitated. "Um . . . I have a new friend. Downstairs. We were going to do our homework together."

His mother raised an eyebrow. "And does your new friend have a name?"

"Niya. Niya Bedford."

His mother smiled. "Your day has been full. That is, what they say, 'fast work,' my son."

"Mother!"

Still smiling, his mother waved him away. "It was always your nature to attract friends quickly. Go. Just remember that your father will be home within the hour, and tired from his first day of work. Supper will be early tonight."

Niya's apartment was as comfortable and clean as Remi's one glimpse had promised. It seemed to be set up the same as his on the floor above: two bedrooms, and from here in the living room he could see into the kitchen, where a half-open door revealed the same sort of small corner room as his own. This was obviously Niya's because of the sign saying ENTER AT OWN RISK. He wondered if her window also overlooked the abandoned rail line. The air was warm from the westering sun against the house's bay-facing side, and Niya had changed into cooler clothes—cooler in both senses of the word. She was barefoot, in thigh-length jean shorts and a blue chambray shirt that made her coffee-toned skin seem to glow. Two top buttons were undone. Remi wished it could have been three, but he tried to tame his eyes. The TV was on, but he wasn't sure what he wanted to see more of, cool American cartoons or this cool American girl.

"Want a Coke, Remi?"

"Oh. Yes, please."

"Well, sit your butt down, boy. I'll get it." Then she paused, looking thoughtful. "Or do you want wine? French kids drink wine, don't they?"

"Well, so I have heard, though Haitians do not think of themselves as being French. I sometimes have wine with meals. It is natural in our society. But I did not think American kids were allowed."

Niya shrugged. "American kids ain't 'allowed' a lot of stuff. Thirty years ago I wouldn't been 'allowed' to use a white bathroom in Mississippi. Just 'cause somethin's a law don't make it right. Anyhow, my mom don't mind if I have a taste now an' then. Course, it prob'ly ain't the kinda wine you used to."

"Well, if you do not mind, I have not had a real Coke in a long time."

"Don't they got Coke in Haiti?"

"It is expensive."

"Well, wine nuthin' special to me, either. Maybe 'cause I know I can have some whenever I want. But Coke's better on a hot day, anyhow."

Remi sat on the edge of the sofa, gazing at the cartoons. The only TV he'd been able to watch in Haiti had been through the barred glass of electronic shops. It seemed a wonder to have one of your own and be free to choose any program you liked.

Niya was back in a moment with two cold cans of Coke. "Want some chips to go with it? How 'bout some cheesy puffs?"

Remi patted his stomach. "No thank you. I am still full from lunch. It seems you can eat anytime you want in America."

Niya grinned. "Sure . . . if you got a gun or some money." She sat down beside him and reached for a schoolbook on the coffee table, then made a face. "So I s'pose we best get this crap capped."

"Um . . . with the TV on?"

"I always do my homework with it on. What's the prob?"

"It just seems a waste."

"Of what?"

". . . Oh. Yes. You are right. Let's get this crap capped."

They worked on math for a while, then

switched to French. Remi tried not to let the TV distract him . . . or Niya's shirt when she yawned and stretched. He shifted his eyes to her watch. "I must go home for supper now."

"Can you come back after? We could watch some more TV."

"Yes. I would like that."

Niya walked him to the door. "So, *au revoir*, Remi."

Remi smiled. "Yes. Later, Niya."

About an hour later Remi was back in Niya's apartment, beside her on the couch, watching TV. His stomach was full once again, though he hadn't eaten much for supper despite the new and tempting American food. Outside the sun was lowering, growing orange as it sank toward the San Francisco skyline across the bay. Niya's watch showed seven-thirty. Remi pointed to the screen.

"What was that?"

"Another commercial. Ronald McDonald."

"Yes, I know the clown, but what was he selling?"

"Huh? What he *always* sellin'—junk food."

"Yes, but I did not *see* any junk food in this commercial."

"Well, everybody know what Ronald McDonald is all about."

"But this is for *children*, Niya. Are you saying that even little children know so well what this clown is selling that actual junk food does not need to be shown?"

"Well . . . I s'pose they do."

Remi shook his head. "That is somehow frightening."

Niya giggled. "Yo! Wanna see somethin' reeeely scary?"

"Such as?"

"Such as the basement."

"Oh. Yes. But I thought you did not go down there at night."

Niya glanced toward the window. "It ain't dark yet. Besides, you'll be with me. Um, so how you say 'ghost' in French?"

"*Fantôme*." Remi grinned. "But it will probably try to scare us in English."

Leaving the apartment, Niya led Remi down the hallway to the rear of the house, where a black plastic garbage can stood beside a door that had heavy locks and bars on its window. But Niya opened another door on the left. There was nothing but blackness beyond. The smells drifting up were familiar enough, those of any old basement: dry rot and dust, dankness in the air, and the damp graveyard scent of a place underground. Remi stepped forward. "Shall I go first?"

"Nah. Better let me. An' watch the steps, they kinda funky." Niya reached past the door frame and twisted a wall switch. A second seemed to pass before a single small bulb came to life down below. Revealed in its dim yellow glow were steep wooden steps, their treads scooped and hollowed from long years of use. They creaked and squeaked as Niya started down with Remi close behind. The air was comfortably cool on Remi's skin, though its scent was of worms and decay. They came to the foot of the staircase. Remi peered around, his eyes getting used to the gloom. The heavy beams overhead were much lower than the ceilings of the upstairs rooms, and were thickly draped with dusty cobwebs.

"Um?" he asked, feeling a little vulnerable in his loose-fitting tank top and knee-length shorts. "Are there things here that bite?"

Niya glanced up. "Black widow spiders,

mostly." She pointed. "There's a big fat one. But they won't bother you if you don't bother them—least, that what my mom always say."

Remi regarded the spider with wary interest, realizing that he would have to learn many more such things, simple, everyday things that any American child would already know. Then he turned to scan the basement once more. The brick walls looked wet in places. The floor was hard-packed dirt, and there was a scatter of the usual junk found in old basements: three-legged chairs, dusty old trunks, a battered table, a ragged mattress, and a few cardboard boxes of unwanted household items. The space was other-wise empty except for a rusty furnace that looked ancient but was probably a lot newer than the house. The dying red glow of last daylight filtered through the one small window, which faced the front yard. The shadows of weeds like skeleton hands seemed etched on its grime-coated glass. The light bulb dangled from wires beside the staircase. A concrete slab had been poured there in the not-too-distant past, and a washer and dryer stood upon it. At least twenty years had gone by since either had left the factory, but his mother would be pleased to have use of them.

Niya appeared at his elbow. "So, how did your mom do the washin' in Haiti?"

"By hand, and not happily."

"That musta sucked."

"I am sure she would agree."

"Well, there's a clothesline in the backyard. I usually hang our stuff out there to dry when the weather's nice. Everything smells better that way. Sheets come out that dryer make you wake up at night dreamin' 'bout dirt."

Remi smiled. "Hence the term *dirt nap* for the dead."

Niya suddenly stiffened. She shot a nervous glance over her shoulder and whispered, "Yo, Remi! Did you *feel* that?"

Remi tensed. He *had* felt something, but he wasn't sure if he should admit it or not. The sensation was strange yet familiar, the spiderweb touch on the back of the neck you felt when being watched. He had experienced it several times in his life: in a patch of dense forest when he'd come upon the ruins of an ancient slave camp, and once in a graveyard outside Port-au-Prince. He fought the urge to spin around, turning slowly instead to face the basement's back wall. "Yesss," he said finally.

Niya seemed more satisfied than scared. "So? What I say? There *is* somethin' spooky down here!"

"Mmm." Remi cupped his chin in one hand and gazed around once more. "It is a very old house. And feeling uneasy is normal when surrounded by darkness and decay. We are people who like the sun and fresh air."

Niya smiled. "That's a cool thing to say."

"Thank you. But it is also true. And as my father would tell you, sensations like this are not always caused by the supernatural. Do you often get such feelings down here?"

"Well . . . no. An' never that strong before." Niya glanced toward the window, which was rapidly darkening. "In the daytime I guess you could say it's just normal-creepy. I usually do the laundry on Saturday mornings. An' I don't stay—just come back to get the stuff when it's done." She turned toward the window once more, now just a dim square of twilight. "One time I lost a sock an' I had to come back down here at night to look for it." She stared toward the rear wall and shivered. "I felt it then! Almost as strong. An'—REMI!"

She had screamed his name and now shrank against him, trembling. Her hand shot out, pointing to the basement's back corner. "LOOK!"

Automatically, Remi had grasped Niya's shoulders as she pressed herself to him. Her body beneath the thin shirt had turned cold. He looked where she pointed, feeling his heart pound in his chest when he seemed to see a dim shape coming out of the wall!

Then he blinked and nothing was there, only Niya still clinging to him and his own arms around her.

"Did you see *that*, Remi?"

Both seemed to realize they were holding each other. They exchanged uncertain looks and separated. Remi stepped past her. "I *thought* I saw something. But, only for a moment."

Niya moved after him and grabbed his arm as if to pull him from danger. "That was plenty long enough for me! Let's get the hell out of here before it comes back!"

But Remi had taken a few more steps toward the corner, and Niya, still holding his arm, came along. Remi murmured, "My father has many books about the supernatural. Some are very old, but all say that there is usually a logical explanation for most of these things." He turned to Niya. "What *exactly* did you see?"

". . . Well, somethin' like a shadow. Comin' out the wall in that corner."

Remi looked around. "There are many shadows down here."

"Yeah, but this was like a shadow *in* shadows. Like a shadow tryin' to come *into* the light. *That* ain't logical, Remi. Shadows run away from the light!"

Her hand on his bare arm was no longer cold, and Remi was finding her touch enjoyable. She followed as he walked to the basement's back wall. In the center was a sort of small alcove, where there was a deeper darkness among the shadows. Rough concrete steps led upward.

"What is this, Niya?"

"I guess it used to be a way to the backyard

from here. Outside there's two wooden doors that angle against the wall. But they're nailed shut an' all covered with blackberry vines."

Remi leaned a little into the opening and peered up. "Yes. I see." He moved on toward the corner. This part of the basement was farthest from the feeble bulb, and the shadows of himself and Niya stretched long and strangely shaped against the crumbling brick. They had almost reached the corner now. Remi stopped and turned toward the distant light. "There are rats down here. I can smell them."

"Well, duh! We're in West Oaktown."

"Yes. But . . ." Remi pointed. "A rat crossing the floor about there, midway between where we stand and the light, maybe sitting up as rats do to see us better, would cast a big shadow in this corner."

"Well . . . yeah . . ." Niya turned to and fro, picturing what Remi had said. "Yeah! Course it would!"

Remi nodded. "So there it is, as my father would say, a logical explanation for what we thought was supernatural."

"Well, damn!"

"I do not understand."

Niya giggled, letting go of Remi's arm. "It was almost gettin' to be fun. Like goin' ghost-bustin'."

"Oh. And I have . . . screwed it all up?"

"Well, it was fun while it lasted. An', tell you the truth, I'm just as happy there ain't no *fantôme* down here for real." She touched Remi's arm again, but more tentatively now, then turned and led him back to the light. Reaching the laundry area, she hopped atop the dryer. "Yo, Remi, you know any *real* ghost stories?"

"Well . . ." Remi glanced back at the corner, then pulled up the strap of his shirt. The air seemed warmer here in the soft pool of light, and he found it almost pleasant to be down in this basement alone with Niya. He climbed onto the washer next to her. "I will tell you a true story."

He drew up his legs and gathered his knees in his arms. "Once, long ago in Haiti, there was a town in the shadow of a volcano. Of course, this town had a French governor, who like most of his kind was stupid and cruel. One day the volcano began to rumble and smoke. Steam rose from cracks in the ground. Only a fool wouldn't have seen the danger, and yet this governor would let no one leave the town. He even stationed his soldiers around the outskirts to keep people from getting away. There were white people, too, but many more black, and in those times we were slaves. Yet it was our people who warned the governor and pleaded with him to let them leave before it was too late. But he remained ever the fool, fearing more to show weakness before slaves than the fiery mountain at his back. Then it came. With no further warning. The eruption! A huge boiling cloud of fire and steam exploded from the mountain and rushed down the slopes faster than the fastest train! Trees and bushes burst into flame the instant it touched them. The town was buried in seconds. All was destroyed, and all were killed, even the governor and his soldiers."

Remi looked over at Niya. She now sat as he did, knees locked in arms, her tawny eyes wide in the dimness. Remi fingered the small wooden cross around his neck. "It is said that the *fantôme* of a slave warned my ancestor of the coming doom. He escaped with his family before the fool of a governor surrounded the town with soldiers.

Since that time we have always had a certain affinity for the supernatural. And it for us."

"Whoa!" breathed Niya. "So I guess you really do know all about ghosts an' hauntin's."

"Well . . ." Remi puffed his chest a little. "I have never experienced a real manifestation. But here I smell only the rat."

Niya glanced toward the shadowy corner, then upward. "My mom should be home now. I better get back."

Remi slid off the washer to help Niya down. "I will walk you to your door and keep the *fantômes* away."

Niya started up the stairs and Remi followed. Niya stepped into the hallway, but Remi stopped with his hand on the light switch. Once more he felt that sensation of being watched.

3

Remi's new clock showed 9:27 as he entered his room. He stripped off his shirt, then sat on the bed to take off his shoes. The day's warmth still lingered, and the small space seemed stuffy. He set his shoes beneath the bed, slipped off his shorts, then knelt on the blankets to examine the window. Yes, it had simply been painted shut over the years and no one had tried to open it. A knife blade and patience would soon solve that problem.

The hoot of an air horn and the distant rumble and clack of steel wheels came to his ears. A train was passing down by the waterfront two blocks away. He watched as the big diesel engine rolled by, then pressed his nose to the glass and gazed up the grass-grown tracks. There were no lights in the scrap yard, and all was in darkness beyond the board fence. Dimly, against the city-glow, he could see the crane booms pointing skyward like spectral fingers. Then he turned his attention back to the sealed window. At the bottom of the sash were two small handles. Taking the clock from the sill and setting it aside, he grasped the handles with both hands and strained upward. Nothing. Sucking a breath, he got a better grip and pulled with all of his strength, head thrown back and teeth bared in a snarl. The small muscles in his chest and arms stood out in stark definition. Suddenly, both handles ripped from the rotten old wood. Remi almost flipped over backward onto the floor. Trying to recover, he pitched forward again, slamming his forehead into the glass. His hands came down hard on the windowsill. A piece of it cracked and broke loose from the frame.

"*Merde*. . . SHIT!"

Remi leaned back, panting. A light sheen of sweat broke out on his body. He dropped one hand to his knee to steady himself, as the other went to rub his forehead. He glared at the window. Fortunately, he hadn't smashed his fool head through the glass and cut his own throat. He looked down at the broken piece of wood now lying on the blanket, then glanced guiltily upward to where the landlady lived on the third floor. True, this was a shabby old house, but it was also his family's first American home and he had no right to damage it. Still rubbing his forehead, he picked up the flat strip of wood. No, he saw with relief, it wasn't really broken. In fact, it didn't look like it had even been nailed. He studied it closer: it *had* been nailed at one time, but the nails had been pulled and for many years nothing but layers of paint had held it in place. Then his eyes focused on the gap in the frame where the sill-piece had been. There seemed to be something metallic inside. Laying down the wood, he bent close and peered into the narrow little space.

There was money!

But, he saw a second later, not much, and only in coins. All thoughts of treasure or a fortune in gold vanished as his fingers quested but captured only a handful of ordinary American coins. He counted them in his palm: three dollars and seventeen cents in time-tarnished nickels, quarters, and dimes, a fifty-cent piece, and a pair of pennies, one green with corrosion and the other . . .

Rusty?

Dropping the other coins on the blanket, he held the second penny up to the light and scanned it carefully. Copper didn't rust. This penny seemed to be made of steel. A counterfeit?

But what criminal would be such a fool as to counterfeit pennies? True, it bore a perfect likeness of the American President Abraham Lincoln. . . . A labor of love, perhaps?

A new hope flared, and Remi examined the other coins once more, but again there was disappointment. The house may have been a hundred years old, but not one of the coins was dated before 1922. The date on the . . . counterfeit? . . . penny was 1943. He had discovered no fortune in antiques, either. Still, he had enough here to treat Niya to a meal at the redheaded clown's after school tomorrow.

Again he bent to peer into the gap. He soon realized that what he had found was nothing more than some child's treasure trove, hidden years past by some other occupant of this room—maybe a boy who watched from this window as a night train puffed past his house. Almost surely a boy, Remi decided, because the next thing he discovered was a small pocketknife. The grips were thick plastic, a good knife by today's standards, and it had been personalized with the name Tom Mix. A truly American name. For the rest, there was only a palmful of papery scraps that might once have been baseball cards. Remi pried open the pocketknife blade. It was stiff and rusty, but still sturdy and sharp. Remi was familiar with blades, and it was clear that Tom Mix had been a boy who cared for his things.

"Remi?" called his mother from the kitchen. "It is late. Time to sleep. Put out the light."

"A moment."

"I will come in."

"I am not clothed!"

"It has not been many years since I have seen you in the wild. Now put out that light or I will come in and do it myself!"

"A moment, is all!"

"A *moment,* then. And good night, my son."

"Good night, Mother."

Remi gathered the coins and put them in a pile on the little night table, then crossed the room and switched off the light. The glow from a street lamp a half block away was enough for him to work at the window frame with the pocketknife blade. After about fifteen minutes he was able to open the sash a few inches. There was a cool breeze off the bay. Carefully, he replaced the sill-piece, then stretched out under his blankets to sleep.

4

The sound of the train woke him . . . rhythmic panting puffs like the breath of some huge jungle beast. . . .

Remi's eyes snapped open to find his room lit daylight bright by glaring electric rays. Could this be the same dream again? He looked at the clock on the windowsill. Its glowing green numbers showed 3:13. This was no dream! How could it be with the whole house shaking beneath him? For a second he almost screamed for his parents. And then he yanked the blankets over his face like a child. Cold sweat sheened his body. He felt his heart hammering in his chest like the thud of those pounding pistons outside. Finally, he forced himself to push off the covers and crouch at the window.

Yes. It was all the same as last night. He squinted straight into the glare of the engine's headlamp, and again it was as if the oncoming train were somehow aware of him. Once more he tensed for a crash, but again the locomotive lurched around the curve at the very last second and puffed slowly past. And again Remi found himself watching a row of low flatcars roll by, rocking and creaking, while steam chilled his body and smoke burned his nostrils and watered his eyes. There as before went the long sheets of steel, the big iron beams, and the massive machinery. And here came the car that carried the great ship's propeller. And there on one blade sat the two shadow-men. Once more Remi saw one reach into his pocket and turn to the other. Slowly, the flatcar rolled past. Remi tried to follow it with his eyes, but the angle was wrong and he quickly lost sight of the men. The window! Grabbing the sash, his small muscles straining, Remi managed to force it open enough to get his head out. The flatcar carrying the propeller had just drawn even with the rear of the house. . . .

Then Remi's eyes went wide in horror. The first man's hand came out of his pocket gripping a gun! There was a flash, bright yellow-orange in the darkness, and the sound of the shot was lost in the clatter and clash of the train. The second man pitched from the flatcar and crashed facedown in the gravel beside the tracks. He lay still. An instant later the other man leaped from the train. Remi watched, frozen, as he took hold of the unmoving shape and dragged it behind the house.

The train chuffed on toward the brilliant arc-lamps of the shipyard. The engine had already entered through a wide-open chain-link gate. A few more flatcars came clanking past, and finally the caboose. Remi watched, still unable to move, as the ruby-red taillight was swallowed in the engine's swirling smoke. And yet this time, unlike the night before, the whole scene outside his window stayed sharp and clear.

It seemed to Remi that time was passing. His clock still stood on the windowsill right by his hand, but he couldn't seem to see it. Moonlight glittered cold and blue on the rails. In the shipyard the train had stopped, and cranes now worked unloading its cargo. Big trucks rumbled to and fro, their headlamps slashing the night. The sapphire sparks of welding torches burned bright as small stars. Voices carried on the breeze, men calling and cursing. Whistles blew, horns honked, and from everywhere came the clanging of steel as a great ship took form in the distance.

And then Remi saw the man come out from behind the house. It was too dark to see his face, but Remi could tell he was tall and lean and that he was wearing dungaree jeans and a heavy denim workman's coat. The man walked onto the tracks as if tired and seemed to rest against something for a moment in order to get his breath back. Then he looked around. Remi felt a cold hand clutch his heart. Would the man see him here at the window? And why did that terrify him so? He still couldn't make out the man's features, except to see that he was white. This brought the realization that the murdered man had been black. Remi wanted to hide, but he still couldn't move. At last the man turned away and began walking up the tracks toward the shipyard. A match flared yellow, and the scent of cigarette smoke drifted to Remi's nostrils on the breeze. He could hear heavy boots crunching gravel.

Then, suddenly, he found he was free of whatever had held him frozen. Leaping from the bed, he yanked on his shorts and dashed from his room. For an instant he considered waking his parents, but no; if they hadn't heard the train, then maybe they weren't meant to. Out in the unlighted hallway, down the dark staircase, and to the back door he ran. He fought a moment with the unfamiliar locks, then burst from the house into icy blue moonlight.

There was dew on the tall grass and weeds, chilly to his feet. Droplets glittered like jewels on the wire clothesline. But now there was only darkness beyond the rickety fence where the ship-yard had been only moments before. Remi scanned the weedy yard but could see nothing that looked like a man's body lying amid the high grass. Near the fence was a tiny, half-collapsed toolshed. Its door hung open on one twisted hinge. His heart pounding again, Remi went to the door and looked in. Moonbeams stabbed through holes in the roof and razored through cracks in the walls. Weeds grew thick between gaps in the floor. But, except for one rusty shovel, a hoe, and a rake, the little structure was empty.

Leaving the shed, Remi now searched the whole of the house's backyard. He was fearful of what he might find, though something inside him wanted to find it. But there was nothing more than an ancient truck tire and two broken lawn chairs. The doors to the basement were boarded up tight and buried by blackberry brambles. There had probably been a flower bed along the back of the house years before, but the untended brambles, chest-high to Remi, had taken control and nothing could get past their long wicked thorns.

Warily, Remi moved on toward the tracks, still scanning the shadowy ground and half-hoping to find what he feared, if only to make some sense of this thing. The fence was mostly fallen, its remains held erect by only the blackberry vines, which seemed to grow thickest at the house's rear corner. At one time there had been a small gate, which was now just a gap in the boards. He passed through. There, before him, were the rails, but it was almost no surprise to find them grass-grown and rusted again. Something stuck up among the dry weeds: the handle and post of a switch. Once, other rails had branched off toward the bay, but now there was only a ghost track in the grass. Remi moved to the switch. Something grabbed his ankle!

He choked back a yell, but then let out a sigh of relief when he saw that he'd just caught his foot in the Y-shaped branching of rails. He touched the switch handle. The ancient iron felt unnaturally cold. The mechanism itself was long rusted solid and would never move again. He studied the alignment of the rails, eternally set to send trains past the house. He cast a last glance toward the mountains of scrap where the shipyard had been, then came back down the tracks to return to his room. About to step off, he stopped to scan the side of the house. There on the ground floor in front was a window that matched his own up above. It had to be Niya's.

And all of this had to be either a dream or something truly supernatural. No one alive could have slept through the passing of the night train. For a moment more he stood there alone in the moonlight. He found himself wondering if the curtains at Niya's window were open and, if so, what he might see if he looked in. He could almost picture her face at peace on her pillow and haloed in moonglow. He saw his own shadow on the fence, a black silhouette with a wild bush of hair. What would she see if she looked out and saw him now? A savage boy from the jungle who prowled half naked in the night? And then he smiled. She had been frightened by a shadow on the basement wall, when the real haunting was going on with a vengeance right outside her window each night!

He was shivering by the time he got back to his room. His feet were dirty, and bits of weeds and grass clung to his ankles and legs. Mindful of waking his parents, he cleaned himself as best he could with a corner of a blanket, then climbed back into bed. The breeze chilled him, and he shut the window and drew the covers up to his neck. Then, just as he closed his eyes, he heard the sound of the train approaching. No! Not again! He almost screamed the words aloud. Once more he wanted to hide, but how could you hide from something that couldn't exist? He lay there, fighting terror. From the corner of his eye he could see his clock, somehow obeying natural laws while everything else had gone mad. It was 4:53 . . . *somewhere*.

He told himself not to watch the train, but the sound was different somehow. Clutching the blankets around his cold body, he rose to peer out the window. The shipyard was there again, but now the train was leaving it, backing down the track. The rays of its taillight bathed the walls of his room in blood. A man was standing on a platform at the rear of the caboose, a lantern glowing yellow at his feet. But Remi didn't want to see any more. Shivering, he lay back down and pulled the covers over his face. He gritted his teeth and squeezed his eyes shut, clutching the little wooden cross in both hands as the ghost train came clanking past his window. Slowly, the sound of it faded in the distance, growing ever fainter like a real train would, until it seemed suddenly gone. Despite himself, he strained his ears to listen but there was nothing; only the sounds of a city in the dead of night. Cautiously, he eased the blanket down. His clock continued flashing the passage of time as if nothing at all had happened. Gradually, the pounding of his heart subsided and his breathing returned to normal. Some of the tenseness left him. He pillowed his head on his arms, staring up at the cracked-plaster ceiling and wondering if he could ever sleep again. Then, surprisingly, a new thought came, that his family now had a refrigerator, and like any American boy he could get up and have a midnight snack. This made him smile. He lay there considering this new possibility and finally sleep came.

5

Niya giggled. "Can't figure why you wanna go to another library. I thought you said you already had a lotta books at home?"

Remi draped his new jacket over one shoulder. The afternoon sun was warm and bright and his tank top was all he needed. The school day had ended, and he and Niya were out on the sidewalk. He carried her books and his own under one arm.

"Yes. But they are not unpacked yet, and I have already read most of them. Besides, none of those we brought from Haiti have any information about Oakland history."

Niya glanced back at the ugly brick school, which to Remi resembled a prison surrounded by barbed wire and mesh. "Well, we spent most of our lunch break lookin' at books."

"Did you mind?"

"Well, no." Niya smiled. "It's just that I never knew a brutha who read books before . . . when he didn't have to." She touched one of the books

Remi carried. "Anyway, I always wanted to read *The Jungle Book*, an' bein' there with you gave me a good excuse to check it out."

Remi smiled, too. "It is a good story. I read it myself years ago. It is good to read about other lands, and of other times. But the school library did not have much information about the history of Oakland."

Niya giggled. "Maybe there ain't much. It ain't like there a *there* here! An' you 'bout gave ole Miz Brooks a cow axin' all those questions!"

"To me she seemed more astonished. No matter. I did learn that Oakland was a major shipbuilding city in the 1940s, and that many of our people came here to work in the shipyards, but I would like to learn more of the details. Anyhow, that book about coin collecting explained the existence of this."

He took the steel penny from his pocket and handed it to Niya. "These were made in 1943. Copper was in short supply because of World War Two."

Niya examined the penny. "Mmm. I never knew that, but I s'pose it makes sense. So, where did you get it?"

Remi hesitated, not sure how Niya would react if he told her of his experiences the night before. "It may prove to be part of a story." Reaching into his pocket again, he brought out the knife and handed it to Niya. "Maybe this, too. I think both must have belonged to a boy named Tom Mix, who lived in our house and probably occupied my room. At least until 1943."

"Why until 1943?"

"There were other coins hidden away with the knife, but none dated later."

Niya nodded. "Mmm." She studied the knife. "Tom musta sent away in one of those comic book ads to get his name put on it. But why would he hide it?"

Remi explained about the windowsill.

Niya nodded again. "Oh yeah. I did somethin' like that when I was eight. Stashed two dollars under a loose board in my room. My dad found it, anyway. He was on crack. He's dead now."

"I am sorry."

Niya shrugged. "Ancient history. Anyway, Tom's folks musta moved out the house pretty fast."

"Why do you say that?"

"Well, three dollars was a lot of money in 1943—I know *that* much about history. Prob'ly almost like twenty today. An' then there's the knife. What I sayin' is, Tom wouldn't just go away an' leave it behind."

"Yes. That makes sense."

"That's another cool thing about you, Remi. You don't figure girls are stupid." Niya grinned. "This is kinda fun. It's sorta like that TV show *Ghost Writer*, where kids go round solvin' mysteries."

Remi's eyes narrowed. "That is very . . . down with it, Niya. Because I am beginning to think that there really is a ghost where we live."

Niya stopped, her own eyes going wide. "Whoa! So, there really *is* somethin' in the basement!"

Remi fingered his jaw, still not sure if he should tell Niya everything, not after what he'd gone through last night. "Well . . . There may or may not be a manifestation in the basement. Or even inside the house. But there is surely a haunting without."

"Without, what?"

"*Outside* the house."

"Whoa!"

"You are not afraid?"

Niya looked around. "Yo. I grew up in this hood, Remi. There's a whole lotta *live* shit to be scared of goin' on all over 'without.' What can dead people do?" She turned back to him. "So? What *is* goin' on? Is Tom Mix floatin' around lookin' for his knife?"

Remi took the knife and slipped it back into his pocket. "I do not see how Tom could have anything to do with the haunting. He was only a boy who was living in the house, at least until 1943. Who he was—or likely still is—should not matter."

Then Remi paused to consider. "Yet it is possible that Tom may have witnessed the . . . incident. That may have been the reason for moving so quickly out of the house that his hidden things were left behind."

Niya cocked her head. "Yo. Don't take much to figure what you mean by 'incident.' This is *me* you talkin' to, Remi. What I sayin' is, if there's a ghost, then you gotta be talkin' 'bout a dirt nap, right? So, just spit it, boy. I'll clue ya when I'm scared."

Remi sighed. "I am sorry. You are right. Yes, I believe there was a . . . dirt nap. But it was outside the house. If Tom had seen, and told his parents, they may have moved immediately, thinking the neighborhood no longer safe."

"Well, this hood don't look like it's gotten no safer in fifty years, for a fact. Course, Tom an' his parents were prob'ly white. White folks can always afford to move where it's safe."

"Mmm. I had not thought of that."

Niya shrugged. "Well, figure that musta been a pretty expensive house at one time. What I sayin' is, it couldn't have always been three separate apartments like it is now." She paused in thought. "Yo, Remi, you down with a whole three-story house just for one family!"

"Amazing. Though I cannot imagine such a house being built on the edge of a railway line. Or next to a shipyard. The . . . hood has probably changed a lot since the house was new. It is possible that it was divided into apartments because of all the wartime activity. Even those few books in the school library said that much of the shipbuilding was done by black men. They and their families would have needed places to live."

"Yeah! So Tom coulda been black."

"Mmm. It is possible. But we will probably learn more about the neighborhood at this library you are taking me to."

"Yeah. It's the Golden Gate one on San Pablo. I been there before. They got this whole room like a museum about Oaktown history. There's even pictures of ships bein' built, an' a lot of our people buildin' 'em, just like you said." Then Niya frowned. "So, what exactly is this 'incident' you talkin' about? You see a *fantôme* last night, or somethin'?"

They had reached a corner bus stop, and now sat down together on the bench. Remi studied Niya again, deciding that he liked her very much. He took a deep breath. "There is a ghost train . . ." he began.

6

It was early evening when Remi and Niya got off a bus and began walking home. Both were silent, thinking. The streets were quiet at this hour: working people were home, and those whom Niya called "zombies" had not yet risen from their alley and doorway graves to trouble the living. A soft breeze carried the scent of the sea and the smells of suppers cooking. Remi sighed. "Black people were treated badly in this country, even though we built many things for the white." He scowled. "The *blanc*."

Niya nodded slowly. "Yeah. It ain't said much in those books, but you can sure feel it."

"And yet we built and sailed those Liberty ships that helped win the war." Remi scowled again. "The war that was supposed to bring 'liberty and justice for all'!" He snorted. "Crimes against us seem to have been given little attention by the police in those times."

"Well, ain't much changed, Remi. In a while

you'll see that yourself." Niya turned to him. "So, ain't we treated badly in Haiti?"

Remi shrugged. "The poor are always treated badly. Their color does not matter much. And being poor in a rich society is always a crime."

"So, you don't figure that blank who killed the brutha on the night train ever got caught?"

"*Blanc.* And my father has told many stories of true manifestations because of unavenged murder. It is one of the really strong factors that may bring on a haunting. If you believe in such things, then it seems only logical that the murdered brother's spirit cannot rest. Hence the *fantôme* train in the night recalling the last moments of his life."

"Well . . . *say* I believe in ghosts, Remi. So, how come I never saw this train? What I sayin' is, we lived in that house for almost five years, an' my own window's right beside the tracks. So, how come all I ever got was spooky feelin's in the basement while you saw the real-live spooks?"

"I do not know. Maybe, as my father has said, I am sensitive to these things. This, too, is often a factor in hauntings." Remi considered. "Or maybe the manifestation can only be seen from the window on the second floor—the window of what is now my room. Did you know the people who lived in the apartment before?"

"It was a older guy an' his wife. No kids. They were okay, but not people me an' my mom got to know very good." Niya smiled. "I never heard 'em talkin' 'bout no trains bumpin' past in the night." She thought for a moment. "Course, I never did see the lady doin' no laundry in the basement. Took her stuff out." Niya snapped her fingers. "Yo! One time she told my mom that washin' come out that basement smellin' like dirt! Just like I told you!"

Remi's forehead creased. "Yes. Smells are often a part of hauntings. Especially those of rot and decay. And dirt."

Niya stopped dead on the sidewalk. "Yo! That's what it is, Remi! That *blanc* sucka buried the brutha in our basement!"

Remi stopped, too, fingering his jaw once more. "It is . . . possible. . . ."

"*Possible?* Yo! Wake up an' smell the dirt, boy! That's gotta be what it is! That's why we saw that shadow comin' out the wall in the corner! It's the brutha's ghost!" Niya spread her palms. "So, all we gotta do now is go dig him up."

Remi's mouth dropped open. "Niya! Are you serious?"

"Well, *course* I'm serious! Ain't that what you do to go settin' some spirit free?" She peered into Remi's face and grinned. "Why you lookin' so *grave*, G?"

Remi frowned. "Because this is a serious thing. If you had seen what I did last night, you would not be making jokes! Besides, I do not see how the murderer could have had time to dig a grave in the basement, even if he did drag the body down there."

"Well, what else could he done with it, Remi? If the body ain't there, then why's our ghost still hangin' around?"

Remi considered. "Well, I suppose we can . . . check out the basement, but even the deepest grave will sink with time. And the shape is unmistakable. We saw nothing like that in the corner yesterday."

"We wasn't lookin' for no grave, Remi."

"True. And the light was very bad."

"So. We'll scope the place out when we get home."

They started walking again. Now it was Niya who fingered her jaw. "Yo, Remi? I was thinkin' 'bout what you said, 'bout your room maybe bein' the only place for gettin' all seven? Those people in the apartment before you prob'ly slept in the big bedroom on the other side of the house, like my mom does."

"Mmm. That makes sense, Niya—no children, and probably no reason to be in that small corner room at three in the morning. Yet could they have been the only people to live there since 1943?"

"Nah. They wasn't old enough. But I never heard nuthin' 'bout whoever cribbed there before."

"What of the landlady on the third floor? She is very old."

"Mrs. Marcus?" Niya made a face. "Believe this, Remi, we ain't gonna get that old cow to talk about nuthin'! Woman look like the Wicked Witch of the West! One time I told her she oughta put a bigger light bulb in the basement 'cause the place was like *Tales from the Crypt*. Maaaan! I thought she was gonna have a instant cow!"

"Um, one can both be a cow and have a cow?"

"Cows can, can't they?"

Remi considered this for a moment. "Oh. Yes."

"Anyway, swear to God, Remi, you dump a bucket of water on that woman, she melt right down to a fizzy little puddle!"

Remi smiled. "I have seen the movie. And I did get that impression of her when we were moving in. Maybe she keeps a small dog locked in a basket upstairs." Then his face turned thoughtful. "But I wonder how long she has lived in the house."

"Yeah. I see what you sayin', Remi. She's plenty old enough to been there in 1943, but I don't think we could ever get her to talk about it."

They had rounded a corner and started down the last block before home, when a small boy of seven or so stepped from a shadowy doorway. He was chocolate brown, very dirty, and miserably thin . . . the raggedest child Remi had yet to see in America. The boy held out his hand, but didn't look very hopeful.

"Can you gimme some money? I hungry."

Remi stopped and looked down at the boy. His own stomach was still full from lunch; he'd had a good breakfast, and could expect a fine supper, plus a midnight snack if he wanted . . . like all American children were supposedly entitled to. Remi dug in his pocket, then gave the boy all the coins he had found last night in the window, keeping just the steel penny. The boy mumbled a rusty-sounding thanks before walking away.

Niya looked puzzled. "Yo. S'up, Remi? Why you lookin' so sad? Ain't there kids in Haiti who beg?"

Remi sighed and walked on. "Many. And there were times when I was one. But Haiti is a very poor country."

Niya took his hand. "Well, you axe me, I think Tom Mix would be proud to know what you did with his money. Wherever he is."

7

"Yo! Just 'cause I'm a girl don't mean I can't dig a grave!"

Remi paused to lean on the shovel. He was shirtless, dirt-streaked, and his ebony body dripped sweat. He stood waist-deep in the ground and looked up at Niya. "If you wish. Though actually we are digging *up* a grave."

"Whatever. Just get outa there an' let me dig awhile."

Remi climbed from the hole and sat with his legs dangling over the edge. Niya took the shovel and jumped down, then went right to work. Remi watched with something like admiration. Niya had dressed for the job in faded old Levi's cut off at the knees, and her blue chambray shirt was knotted to bare a chocolate-brown middle that Remi found charmingly padded with puppy-chub. The shirt was otherwise unbuttoned, and grew damp and loose as she dug. Remi pulled his eyes away and glanced toward the small basement window. The last light of day was fading beyond.

Almost two hours had passed since they had come down here. Niya had brought a candle, and they had carefully scanned the floor in this corner, discovering a sinking about the right shape and size for a grave. And yet Remi was doubtful. The whole basement floor was far from level and had shifted and sunk everywhere. But Niya had been determined to dig up a ghost, and the old shovel they found in the toolshed had still been in good enough shape to use.

Remi's eyes returned to the girl. The rays from the light in the laundry area hardly reached over here. Niya's candle now burned in an old forty-ounce bottle beside the mounting pile of freshly dug dirt, its soft golden glow casting flickering shadows over her face.

"Um, Remi? You figure he's all gone to bones by now? What I sayin' is, I seen a real *new* body on my way home from school last year, an' I don't think I'd get freaked by just a *old* skeleton, but I ain't sure I wanna see nuthin' in between."

Remi smiled. "After all this time I am sure there

will be only bone." Then he added, "If anything at all."

"You sayin' even bones might be rotted away by now?"

"That is not what I am saying. The deeper we dig, the more doubts I have."

Niya paused in her digging to lean on the shovel and look up at Remi. She wiped sweat from her forehead with the back of her hand. Droplets glittered like gold in her hair, and her skin glistened warmly. "So, what is it you sayin'?"

"Well, remember that the ghost train passed my window at three-thirteen? Even if we allow for the time when I could not seem to move, that still leaves no more than a half-hour for the murderer to bury the body."

Niya glanced down at her feet. "But you told me the train came back about five o'clock."

"Four fifty-three."

"Okay. So that's over a hour an' a half."

"Yes. But also remember that I saw the *blanc* come out from behind the house, go onto the tracks, pause a few moments at the switch, and finally walk up the line toward the shipyard. Then it took me about fifteen minutes to search the backyard and go onto the tracks, and then it was at least another quarter-hour from the time I returned to my room until the train came past again, unloaded and backing up."

"Well, that's still a hour, Remi. After all, you told me you didn't look at your clock before you ran downstairs. So you don't really know how long you was there at the window."

"Mmm. True. And as I said, math has never been one of my favorite subjects."

Niya grinned. "Yeah? So just hope your life never depends on it someday!" She began digging again, leaving Remi to ponder the problem. Her shirt came undone and fell open. She gave Remi a glance from the corner of her eye as she retied it. "Boys are so lucky."

Remi politely looked away. "Are we? That is news."

"Course. You get all hot an' sweaty, you can just take off your shirt."

"You may."

Niya giggled. "Oh, suuuure! You'd like that, wouldn't ya?"

"Well, I would not mind. But I think you are beautiful, with clothes or without."

"Yeah? So, how would you know about the 'without'?"

Remi smiled. "I have seen much already that is beautiful about you."

Niya looked down at herself. "Well, my mom says I should be wearin' a bra. I got one, but it's the most goddamn uncomfortable piece of . . . *merde* anybody ever invented!"

"I can *almost* imagine."

Niya smiled. "I like when you called me beautiful. No other boy ever called me that."

"Maybe another word? A cool American one meaning the same?"

"I like the uncool one better. How do you say it in French?"

"Well, I would say *délicieux*."

"That sounds better than cool. *Merci*."

"You are welcome."

Niya's smile turned shy. "I like the way you're lookin' at me now—sorta respectful. Some G-boy would prob'ly be schemin' how to jump my bones right here in this grave."

Remi shrugged. "I cannot deny that I like what I see. But there are still many parts of Haiti in which the sight of a woman's breast is a natural thing and does not make every man scheme about jumping bones."

Niya looked thoughtful. "I guess people's bodies *are* kinda natural things, huh?" She studied Remi. "Well, I think you're delicious, too."

Remi looked down at his own body. The top button of his shorts had popped open under a tummy that seemed a lot rounder than it had been only two days before. "It is far too easy to eat in America when you are not really hungry."

Niya smiled. "I like your shape, Remi. It's sorta . . . well, cuddly."

Remi sighed and patted his stomach doubtfully. "Another week and I will probably look as if I have swallowed a basketball. It has something to do with metabolism, I suppose. And all this rich American food."

"I don't know what you figure so 'rich' about beans and rice," said Niya. "Were you raised in the jungle or somethin'?"

Remi smiled. "My father sometimes asks me that, adding 'by stupid wolves.' There were times when we thought it wiser to live with relatives in the countryside than to stay in the city. Freedom to speak your mind seems also a natural thing, but there are people who scheme to take even that freedom away."

"You sayin' your dad had to hide? Go underground, sorta?"

"Sort of. There are those who do not respect natural things."

Niya smiled again. "I do got pretty good breasts, huh?"

"Kickin' *totalement*."

"Well, y'all can keep lookin' at me respectful while I'm diggin' some more."

"That may not be necessary."

Niya looked surprised. "Why?"

Remi pointed to Niya's watch. "It comes back to the factor of time. We are both young and strong, and have been digging for almost an hour. You stand now up to your delicious navel, and still we have found no bones. The dirt here is hard-packed and not easy to dig. It would have been so even in 1943. Given the strength of desperation, a grown man might be able to dig a grave in softer ground in about half an hour, but I do not think so down here. I would say that even if the murderer had had a full hour, he could not have dug any deeper than we and still have had time to fill in the grave and hide what it was."

Niya looked around. "Well, did he *have* to hide it? What I sayin' is, nobody comes down here much."

"*Today*, maybe. But it is logical to assume that those doors to the backyard were useable in 1943, if for no other reason than the murderer would hardly have tried to drag a body through the house. There may not have been a washer and dryer in those days, but the original furnace probably needed more attention than this one. What I am saying is, it would have been all but impossible for a shallow grave to pass unnoticed for long in this corner."

Once more Niya leaned on the shovel. "But it's *got* to be here, Remi! This corner is where the *feelin'* comes from! An' the shadow came out that wall! Can you have a ghost without a body? . . . Um, well, you know what I sayin'?"

Remi shrugged. "It is the unresting spirit that does the haunting, not restless bones."

"But what keeps the spirit *here*, Remi?"

"Maybe I will unpack my father's books this evening and dig there for an answer."

"Why don't you just axe him? You said he was a expert on this stuff."

Remi hesitated, then scuffed at the dirt with the toe of his Nike. "Well, this is my first real ghost, Niya."

"*Our* ghost."

". . . Yes. But my father has many living-world worries right now, and I do not want to trouble him with those of the dead."

Niya looked slightly skeptical, but sighed. *"Boys!"* She wiped her face with the tail of her shirt, then studied her hands. *"Merde!* I'm gonna get a blister! Shoulda wore my mom's work gloves."

Remi examined his own palms. "Me, too."

Niya smiled. "Most boys wouldn't admit that. Wouldn't be G."

"I am not a G-boy. I am my own boy, and my ass is tired." Remi sighed and got to his feet, then offered Niya a hand. "I think we have been trying to dig up the shadow of a rat. I will start filling in the grave. Let us hope it passes unnoticed. I do not like police." He took up the shovel and began refilling the hole. Niya watched him awhile, then wiped more dirt and sweat from her body with the shirttail. Remi smiled, still working. *"Délicieux."*

"Well, they could be bigger, but not too much. Like I said, bras suck!" Niya faced him. "I s'pose you ran around buck-naked in Haiti? I can even sorta picture you in the jungle, all shinin' with sweat an' swingin' one of those great big machete knives."

Remi snorted. "You are picturing my ancestor as a boy, harvesting sugarcane for his *blanc* master. Also see that this boy wears a leather mask locked on his face so that he must go hungry surrounded by food." He scowled and slapped his stomach. "I am sure he did not worry about *his* shape!" Then Remi's face softened once more. "I have used a machete, but not often naked. Bushes and thorns are not kind to 'natural' boys."

"Well, at least you don't got to put up with periods." Niya tugged her shirt tighter around her as the night chill seemed to seep through the crumbling brick walls. "Yo. We can drag that old mattress over here to cover the diggin'."

"Good idea."

"So? What we gonna do now, Remi? About the . . . manifestation?"

Remi shoveled more dirt. "I am not trying to be a . . . smart-ass, Niya, but it seems that I am the only one being haunted."

"Yo! Just 'cause I can't see the ole spook train don't mean I'm down with it puffin' past my window! Or knowin' that some poor brutha's gettin' dirt-napped every night at three-thirteen! You tellin' me you outa ideas?"

"But what can 'we' do if it is only I who can see the ghost train?"

Niya thought for a moment, then smiled. "I'm stayin' with you tonight."

The shovel slipped from Remi's hands. *"What?"*

"Yo! It makes total sense. What I sayin' is, if you can only see the train from your window, then I got to be there with you. Chill out. It's Friday, so there's no school tomorrow." Niya smiled. "Besides, you a 'natural' kinda boy, remember?"

"Well . . . yes. But I was raised properly. My parents would be shocked. And my mother would have an instant cow."

"So, what time they go to bed?"

"About eleven."

"Okay, then. I'll be out in the hall by your door at midnight. You let me in an' we wait in your room. Maybe there ain't nuthin' we can do about the ghost train, but at least I wanna see it."

Remi slid the last shovelful of earth onto what was now a disturbingly grave-shaped mound. Beyond the basement window was only blackness. "All right, Niya, we are . . . up for it. Here. Take my hand. We will tramp down this dirt and then get the mattress."

Niya took Remi's hand, then studied it. "You really did get a blister."

"Well, duh."

She kissed it. "Better?"

"Much. Come."

Hand in hand, they jumped on the mound, flattening it a little, then crossed the room and dragged the decrepit old mattress into the corner. They were laying it down when a shadow rose up on the wall!

Remi gasped and grabbed Niya. The shadow darkened and grew, taking shape. . . .

"What are you children doin' down here?"

Remi and Niya both spun around. There stood the old landlady, hands on her hips and fury on her face. Remi's mouth moved but no sound came out. It was Niya who first found her voice.

"N-not what you prob'ly thinkin' right now."

The old woman's eyes ran down Remi's sweat-slicked body, noted the shorts low on his hips with a button undone, then flicked to Niya's half-open shirt, then to the candle, and then to the mattress. She looked about to explode.

"You . . . you . . . HORRIBLE children! You . . . *nasty* . . . *wicked* . . . DIRTY little trash! GET OUT OF HERE!"

Clutching Niya's hand, Remi drew her wide around the furious old woman. "Um . . . we are sorry, madame. But—"

"*Get out!* . . . Just no decency left in this world! . . . OUT!"

Remi and Niya dashed for the stairs.

8

"Remi! Come here!"

"Mother! I am in the bath!"

"Remi! This instant!"

With a reluctant sigh, Remi sat up in the bathtub. It was a huge claw-footed thing that held almost enough water to float a Liberty ship. A hot bath whenever he chose was another American luxury, and Remi had been lounging like an aristocrat after scrubbing the basement dirt from his body.

"Remi! Must I come in and take you by the ear?"

Wondering why his mother sounded so angry, Remi climbed from the tub and wrapped a towel around his waist, then, dripping wet, went into the kitchen. His parents were at the table, cups of coffee before them. His father looked thoughtful, his mother furious.

"Ah! Here he is! The *enfant sauvage!* The wild

child straight from the jungle! Remi DuMont, you are a horrible boy!"

"*Huh?*"

His father indicated a third cup of coffee. Remi sat down at the table, one hand holding the towel.

"And what have I done?"

"Do not play innocent with your mother! Madame Marcus has spoken to me!"

". . . Oh."

"How *could* you, not three days in America, attempt a liaison in the basement with Mademoiselle Bedford?"

" *What?* We did no such thing!"

"Was not there a mattress, a candle, and you naked to the world like the savage thing you are?"

"Oh, shi— Nonsense! I was no more 'naked' than I am right now! *Less* naked! And Madame Landlady is an evil-tempered old . . . *cow* with a dirty mind!"

Remi's father sipped coffee to hide a smile. "I may agree, my son. But remember that we are at her mercy. Large apartments like this are not easily found for what we can afford."

Remi's mother was still scowling. "And so

what *were* you and young Niya doing down there?"

Remi thought fast. Not once in his life had he ever lied to his parents. "Niya was showing me the washing machine . . . and the dryer."

"Oh? And so of course you had to disrobe to test them?"

"There was no disrobing! I . . . just took off my shirt. There are black widow spiders, and one . . . could have crawled down my neck."

His mother rolled her eyes. "And so the two of you were lounging on a mattress watching spiders by candlelight? How could you have forgotten the wine in such a romantic setting?"

Remi frowned. "Madame Marcus exaggerates. We were not upon any mattress." He faced his mother and added, "It is true we had planned a liaison, but it will take place tonight in my room."

"Remi! Do not become the American boy with your mother! We have gone through much hardship as a family, yet we have always maintained our honor."

Remi blew out a sigh but nodded, then turned to his father. It would be easy now to tell him about the manifestation and ask advice—an easy way out of this silly little mess. But what if his father wanted no part of a house with a haunting? What if he decided they had to move? Remi thought of Niya. Maybe it was selfish, but he wanted to stay. And maybe together they could somehow get rid of the ghost train.

"We . . . were exploring the basement. There is only one light, and so Niya brought a candle. We *moved* an old mattress. . . ." Remi glanced at his mother. "It was rotten and nested with rats. Surely you do not think we would lie upon such a thing?" He got to his feet, one hand on the towel, and faced his father again. "I am sorry the landlady misunderstood. But there is no more to the matter than what I have said."

His father placed a hand on his shoulder and sat him gently back down. "That you and Mademoiselle Bedford were just looking at the laundry machines and 'exploring' the basement?"

". . . Yes. It is . . . ghostly down there."

His father looked thoughtful once more. "Yes, I imagine it is in a house as old as this one."

His mother gave Remi a long look. "And so this was *truly* all the two of you were doing?"

Remi tugged at the towel. "Little more than that."

His mother regarded him for another moment, then finally nodded. "Very well. But you must make amends with Madame Marcus. And instantly! You have honor, and it is beneath you to let anyone question it."

"But what can I do? That woman is such a formidable—"

"*Vache* . . . Cow." His father seemed to enjoy the English word, and smiled again. "Maybe. But I think an apology would work wonders. Madame Marcus seems very lonely. And she is old. I imagine that American children were more polite in her time. Maybe also an offer of service?"

Remi nodded, a little reluctantly. "I suppose. But in what way?"

His mother clicked her tongue. "Have you seen the backyard? It is a jungle out there! You have dealt with worse."

"You are saying I should cut weeds?"

"Is that a task beneath an American boy?"

Remi sighed. "No. All right, I will offer my service to Madame *Vache*." He glanced down at his tummy and muttered, "No doubt it will be good exercise."

His mother nodded once more, then gave him a smile. "No doubt it will. American girls seem to prefer 'buffed' young men."

Remi also smiled. "You have been watching too much TV."

After supper, in clean khaki shorts and a white shirt buttoned up to the neck, he climbed the steps to the third floor. The air in the unlighted stairwell was musty and stale with the scent of old woodwork and cobwebs. It was only the smell of all ancient houses, somehow lonely and sad, but here it was stronger, as if the old woman had gathered it around her through the years. Arriving at the landlady's door, he knocked.

From inside came the squeak of a chair, a shuffle of slippers, and finally the harsh iron rattle of bolts being drawn. The door creaked open a crack, and then to the width allowed by its chain. The old woman's face was framed in the gap, dark and wrinkled and dour. A sudden strange look, almost of fear widened her eyes for a moment, then they narrowed and glared out at him.

"What you want, boy?"

Remi put on his brightest smile, as he had for the tourists around Port-au-Prince. "Madame, Mrs. Marcus, I come to apologize for the . . . incident this evening."

The woman considered him, her expression like God regarding a dubious creation. "Mmm. Can't say your folks didn't teach you some manners. At least." Her eyes lingered on his face, almost seeming to search it for a second before turning fierce once again. "You on drugs, boy?"

"Certainly not, madame!"

Once more the eyes softened slightly, as if it took effort to keep them obsidian-hard. "Mmm. Well, this ain't no cathouse, boy, so knock off the 'madams.' We say 'ma'am' in this country when respectin' our elder women."

"Yes . . . ma'am. And, as I say, I am sorry to have upset you today. Mademoi— Niya Bedford and I meant no harm in your basement."

Something like the ghost of a smile tugged at the old woman's lips for a moment. "An' of course you meant no 'harm' to Miss Bedford?"

"No, ma'am."

"Well, what about that mattress?"

". . . We were chasing a rat."

The woman studied him again. "Mmm. Can't say there's any shortage of 'em down there." She shrugged. "Well, it'll be interestin' to see if you still so polite after a month or two in this neighborhood. I don't want no kids messin' round in my basement. Been livin' with rats all my life, but I let you children run wild, an' next thing I know the place be full of winos an' junkies like all the other houses round here."

"Yes, ma'am." Then Remi had a thought. "Is that why the doors are nailed shut?"

For the briefest instant the old woman's eyes tried to harden, but then gave up the struggle and seemed to go sad. "Yes. But I had that done years ago, boy. *Years* an' years ago. Used to think this neighborhood was rough in them days, but it just gone from bad to worse!" She studied Remi for another moment, then sighed, sounding tired. "Okay, son. You done said you're sorry, an' I do believe you are. I could see you was good people, otherwise you wouldn't've got the apartment. Just leave the rats be." She started to close the door.

"Um, Mada— Mrs. Marcus?"

The door stopped closing. "Yes, son?"

"I have seen all the blackberry vines over-growing the backyard."

The door opened to the width of its chain once again. "Yeah. Once them things root, you never get rid of 'em." The woman's face took a distant look now. "S'pose I only got myself to blame. Planted 'em in 'forty-one . . . just a few at the corner of the house . . . but two years later they was all over the fence an' growin' like gang-busters." She smiled now, faintly. "My husband, Jeffery, he loved blackberry pie. So did our son, Randolph . . . Randy . . ."

Her voice trailed off, and she gazed at Remi once more. "You remind me of him . . . Randy. Got 'bout the same build—fine bones, nice features, dark as a panther he was. Polite an' well-mannered, too. Course, Randy couldn't speak French."

Remi sensed sadness. "And . . . what of them?"

Mrs. Marcus sighed, her gaze going to the unlighted stairwell. "War took Jeff." She seemed about to say more, but then her eyes returned to Remi. "Never could abide blackberry pie after that. Had me this house to run. We bought it cheap right after the shipyard went in an' they laid down them train tracks so close. Was Jeff's idea—buy it and make three apartments. Said we couldn't lose with all the new workers an' their families pourin' into Oakland to build them ships. White folks couldn't get out fast enough, but it still took every last bit of our savin's. Turned out Jeff was right; ground floor rented the same day we put up a sign. Randy was in seventh heaven in this house; had his very own room for the first time in his life. He helped Jeff do the carpentry work—good at carpentry, he was, just like his father."

She stopped to study Remi again. "Well, I don't expect you're interested in all that."

Remi's smile was genuine now. True, he had come here only because his mother insisted, but the landlady no longer seemed formidable or frightening. "But I *am*, Mrs. Marcus! I want to learn about this house."

Mrs. Marcus hesitated, then smiled. "Would you like to come in?"

"Yes. I would like that."

It was as if he had stepped back in time when he came through the door. The apartment was small, hardly more than a garret shaped by the slope of the roof. The living room was also half kitchen, and cluttered with old-fashioned furniture mostly made of dark wood and covered with brocaded cloth. Everything was spotless yet sadly aged. The only light came from a tall brass floor lamp with a faded gold shade. It cast a glow over an armchair and an end table beside it on which stood several photographs in tarnished gilt frames. A book also lay there, its place marked with a scrap of red ribbon. Except for a few current magazines and an *Oakland Tribune* on a glass-topped coffee table, the only thing that looked even remotely new was a small TV sitting atop a huge cabinet radio. An open doorway revealed a single small bedroom, and another a tiny bath. A gabled window, its lace curtains drawn, overlooked the backyard. Mrs. Marcus fastened the locks behind Remi. "I don't s'pose you'd like some tea?" she asked.

"Oh, yes please, ma'am."

"Just about to make some. I'm sorry, son, what's your name?"

"Remi."

Mrs. Marcus smiled. "I won't be a minute, Remi. Make yourself at home." She went to the kitchen area.

There was a big sofa beside the lamp-lit chair. Remi walked over to it but stopped to study the pictures on the table. There were three, all black-and-white now faded to gray. The one in the middle was of a young and smiling Mrs. Marcus and a well-built young man with his arm around her. With them was a dark, slender boy who looked about ten. The photo on the left showed the same man, slightly older, more serious now, and wearing a chambray shirt like Niya's, seaman's dungarees, and white sailor's cap. The last photo was of the boy. He, too, looked older here, about Remi's age, and stood shirtless and grinning in front of the backyard toolshed. He was small-chested but round-tummied—a gentle cartoon-kid shape—his own dungaree jeans clinging low like today's baggy hip-hop styles. Their cuffs were turned up above old-fashioned black-and-white sneakers. He held a shovel in one hand.

Mrs. Marcus returned with two china cups and saucers. She handed one to Remi, then followed his gaze to the photos. A smile touched her lips once again, and her eyes shone warm in the lamplight.

"That was my Jeff an' Randy. In the middle there's when we first moved into this house. Jeff was so proud. Wasn't many of our people owned their own homes in them days, an' scant few fine as this one . . . even if it was up next to a railroad track. That other one's Jeff the day before he sailed. An' there's Randy again, wearin' his daddy's ole jeans. Thin as a rail, that boy was when we first moved in here. But we started makin' money, an' with all my good cookin', he put some meat on his bones in no time. Had him a thing for raidin' the icebox at night, too." Her smile widened. "Don't let that grin of his fool you. Seemed like the one thing in this world he couldn't abide was dirt. Diggin' it, anyway. He'd do anythin' else for me, but I had to stand over that boy with a whip just to get him to dig a few weeds. That was him in 1943. I'd sent him out to tame down them brambles. . . ."

Mrs. Marcus turned from the pictures. "Lord, here I am forgettin' my own manners! Sit yourself down, son. An' for heaven sake, unfasten that collar, y'all look about ready to strangle."

Remi sat on the edge of the sofa, balancing the

saucer on his knee and gratefully unbuttoning his tight shirt collar, while Mrs. Marcus sank into her chair.

"Y'all was askin' 'bout them blackberries. Guess I just let 'em run wild. Long's I can keep a path clear to the clothesline, I don't pay 'em no mind. If you was talkin' 'bout the berries themselves, won't be none till July or so. You an' your family be welcome to 'em, course, but I should warn you Mrs. Bedford tried to bake a pie with 'em first year she moved in an' it didn't turn out very good. Guess they ain't sweet like they used to be. I'd soon see 'em gone, but it'd cost a fortune to get 'em dug out now."

Remi took a sip from his cup. "Well, I was going to ask if you would like me to clear them away."

Mrs. Marcus cocked her head. "Now, why would you wanna do that?"

"In apology for what happened today. And to prove myself useful."

The old woman smiled. "You really are somethin' else, son." She hesitated. "But I can't give y'all no break on the rent."

"That is not necessary. It will be a pleasure to help."

"A 'pleasure,' huh? That'd been about the last thing my Randy would've called diggin' dirt!" Mrs. Marcus turned to gaze at the pictures once more. "Always dreamin' 'bout goin' to sea, Randy was. Just like his father in one of them ships they was building out there."

"Mr. Marcus sailed on a Liberty ship?"

The woman's eyes saddened. "He was lost on one—'presumed lost,' the government letter said. I kept hopin' for years afterward it wasn't true. Used to have me this dream, over an' over, that he'd been rescued by another ship. A foreign one that took him to some faraway place, but he was on his way home."

Remi saw that the old woman's eyes were glistening in the lamplight. He set his cup and saucer down gently. "And your son, Randy?"

Mrs. Marcus sighed, still gazing at the photographs. "He . . . followed his father, I suppose. Always wantin' to go to sea, but I wouldn't have none of it. Woke up one mornin' an' he was gone. He was only thirteen, but the merchant service was takin' 'em young in them days . . . desperate for men . . . signin' on sixteen-year-olds. Him bein' black, prob'ly wasn't many questions asked. That boy was always brave as a lion. . . ." She pulled a handkerchief from the pocket of her dress and dabbed at her eyes. "It was only a week after that picture was taken. That's been the worst of it, son—all these years an' never really knowin' whatever become of 'em."

Remi got quietly to his feet. "I am sorry, Mrs. Marcus."

The woman sighed again. "It's all right, son. It was a long time ago. You're a good young man to even sit here and listen to me."

"I must go now. But I would like very much to come visit again. And thank you for the tea."

Mrs. Marcus rose, wiped her eyes, and slipped the handkerchief back into her pocket. "Well, you wanna tackle them brambles, that's fine with me. Don't know what y'all plannin' to use for tools—nothin' but rusty ole junk in what's left of the shed, an' I can't afford no new shovel."

"I will manage."

"Well, ya'll best get yourself a good heavy pair of gloves at least. Them thorns still sharp as they was fifty years ago, rip your hands right to shreds."

Mrs. Marcus unlocked the locks and opened the door. Remi stepped out into the hall, then paused. "Um, was there ever a family named Mix in this house? With a son named Tom?"

The woman looked at him strangely. "Son, are you messin' with me?"

Surprised, Remi stepped back a pace. "Certainly not!"

Mrs. Marcus eyed him for a moment in what almost seemed like suspicion, but then finally she shrugged. "No. Never no family named Mix in this house." She shut the door and the locks rattled back into place.

9

You figure she seen the ghost train?" Niya asked in a whisper.

Remi shook his head. "I did not ask, but I am sure she has not. I have seen it twice now, and once was more than enough! I cannot imagine anyone living with such a fearsome thing for over fifty years."

He and Niya lay on his bed, he at the head, she at the foot. Both had their arms crossed under their heads and their legs drawn up, their Nikes and Cons touching toes. Remi had shed his white shirt and now wore his bulky blue jacket, half unzipped in the warm night air. Niya had on faded Rye jeans and a huge black hoodie.

She glanced at the clock, which showed 2:57, and then at her watch. She had brought her library book, a candle, and a small bottle of Night Train wine, "boosted," she'd said, from her fridge at the price of a scolding tomorrow. She had grinned when Remi saw the label and looked shocked. The window was open, and the candle flickered on the sill in the sea-scented breeze, filling the room with a soft golden glow. Remi had read to Niya from the book, whispering the story of Mowgli the jungle boy from another place and time. Now they were sipping the wine from paper cups.

"So," Niya whispered, "what makes you figure the ghost train been comin' by for fifty years?"

Remi also glanced at the clock. His body seemed stiff with tension. "Well, it is only a feeling I have, but I believe that I saw the train as Tom Mix did . . . as the boy who watched from this window. And the coins set the date of his being here no later than 1943."

"But you told me that Mrs. Marcus said there wasn't never no family named Mix in this house."

"I have been trying to figure this out, though as I said, she seemed surprised when I asked about Tom Mix."

Niya thought for a moment. "Well, there might not be a 'Niya Bedford' no more if my mom ever gets married again."

"Mmm. True. Or Mix may have been a family that caused Mrs. Marcus trouble, maybe one she had to evict and has bad memories about." Remi tapped the windowsill with a fingertip. "An eviction might also explain why Tom left his treasures behind." He flicked another glance at the clock, which now showed 3:01. "At least it is almost certain that Tom was black, because it would have been unlikely that black and white families would share the same house in 1943."

"Still ain't likely," said Niya. She was cleaning the "grave dirt" from under her fingernails with the blade of Tom's knife. She, too, kept flicking glances at the clock. "Can you hear it comin'? Like the real trains down by the water?"

"I have been asleep both nights until it was very near."

Niya cocked her head toward the window and listened. There was only the far-off rumble of freeway traffic, a distant siren wailing, and what might have been a gunshot, a sound that Remi sadly recalled from his homeland.

Niya took another sip from her cup and gazed out at the stars. "I read in my science class book that some of those stars are so far away that their light took a million years to get here. An' some of 'em are already dead, but their light keeps on shinin'. Kinda strange, huh? Almost like they was ghost stars."

Remi smiled. "Yet to us they still seem very alive. And just as beautiful."

Niya fiddled with her cup for a moment. "Um, Remi? You ever kissed a girl?"

". . . Um . . . no. Have you ever kissed a boy?"

". . . No."

Remi felt somehow relieved. "Maybe one day we may . . . check that out." Then he looked at the clock again, his stomach tightening as the green numbers changed to show 3:09. "But not tonight."

Niya followed his eyes. "No. Not tonight." She set down her empty cup beside Remi's, folded the knife, and laid it on the sill.

"Put it in your pocket," said Remi.

Niya picked up the knife once more. "Somethin' I should know?"

"I am not sure. It is true that I have had no actual experience in these matters, but I just had a thought. Suppose Tom *did* witness the murder from this window. Maybe I was seeing it through his eyes because his things were so near."

"You mean like those psychic people who pick up vibrations from stuff?"

"Yes. Things like that can be important factors in manifestations, even allowing them to happen. It can be like adjusting a radio."

"Yeah! I hear you, Remi. It's like the station's always there, but you gotta tune it in."

"Yes. I have the steel penny in my own pocket. If you take Tom's knife, then maybe we will both see the ghost train."

"Mmm." Niya slipped the knife into her jeans pocket. "It almost makes sense."

"Remember, Niya, we may be entering a place where what makes sense as we know it makes no sense at all. I looked through some of my father's books, but there are many things I do not understand about this manifestation. It seems somehow more complicated than just a simple haunting by a ghost. My father has often suggested that even the supernatural must follow logical laws, but they are not the laws of this life, and so may confuse and even endanger the living."

Then Remi stiffened and jerked upright on the bed. "A train!"

Niya turned to the window, her expression unsure as if she wanted to deny the distant rumbling sound now that she actually seemed to be hearing it. "Well, we already heard two tonight . . . real ones."

Remi grasped her hand. *"Listen!"*

She, too, sat up straight, leaning toward the window, her own hand tightening on Remi's. "Yeah! It's . . . *different!* Like the ones in ole movies!" She pointed. "*There!* You can see the light! An' the smoke! It's three-ten Remi! It's really *comin'!*"

Both scrambled to their knees, crowding each other at the window. Two blocks down, the huge iron beast came chuffing around a line of dimly seen buildings and lurched with squealing wheels onto the track that led up the street. Remi and Niya squinted their eyes as the fierce blue-white headlamp shone full in their faces. Niya leaned out the window.

"The shipyard, Remi! It's *there!* Where the junkyard used to be! I can *see* it!"

But Remi grabbed Niya's shoulder and pulled her back inside. "Be careful, Niya! Remember, it may be dangerous to try and take part in something that has already happened! And do you not feel as if the train itself is some-how aware?"

Niya's eyes widened. "You sayin' it can see us, that the murderer might even be able to see us?"

"I do not know! But never forget this thing has *already* happened! Fifty years ago! Maybe we can only watch, as Tom may have watched, and do nothing to change it. But I knew Tom's fear last night! It *was* fear that the murderer would see him!"

The engine was nearing, all smoke and fire and spewing steam, its signal bell clanging, its great wheels grinding steel upon steel. Remi blew out the candle. Niya took his shoulders, shouting above the gushing of steam and the ground-shaking rumble of hundreds of tons of on-coming iron:

"But we could *try* an' do somethin' to change it, Remi! What would that hurt? Maybe it would only be like tryin' to change the endin' of a movie, but we could *try*! We could try an' warn the brutha to watch his back!"

"But Tom did not do that!"

"Tom didn't *know* what was gonna happen! We do! Remi, we *gotta* try!"

With smoke billowing black against the night sky and massive wheels locked to the rails that guided them, the train took the curve that would carry it past the house. Steam poured through the window, soaking their faces and hair. Before he could stop her, Niya leaned out the window and began shouting at the locomotive. Remi pulled himself out beside her and yelled and waved, too, but, as before, the engineer was only a shadow backlit by boiler-flame glow. There was no sign that the figure had seen them. His profile just leaned from the cab, intent on the track straight ahead. And now the engine was past, and now came the line of low flatcars. Nothing had changed.

Smoke in his eyes, Remi saw the steel plates, iron beams, machinery. And then came—

"LOOK OUT!" Remi screamed to the black man on the propeller blade. "HE WILL KILL YOU!"

Then Remi could only watch in horror, and a flick of his eyes showed that Niya's expression was the same. Passing in shadow below, the white man reached into his pocket.

Remi took Niya's hand, holding it tight as the murderer brought out the gun. And again, the sound of the shot was lost in the clatter and clash of the train.

Remi tried to pull Niya inside, to keep her from seeing what would follow. But she was strong and stayed to watch as the black man's body was dragged out of sight. It was all the same. . . .

But no! Something *had* changed! For a second, Remi didn't know what it was—not the scene, or the shipyard, or the fading red lamp on the back of the train. . . . He could *move!* He was no longer frozen in time like he'd been the night before!

He drew back inside, and Niya came with him now. She was sobbing. He held her, both kneeling against each other on the bed. She buried her face on his chest, her tears warm on his skin.

"I never seen it *happen* before! Everybody talks about it, gettin' capped, but I never seen it happen for real! It's over so fast! One second you're alive, an' then it's nuthin'!"

Time crept by. They stayed together like that, holding each other. At last Niya sank back against the wall, facing away from the window. "Is it still goin' on out there?"

One glance was enough. "Yes. The rails, the shipyard. You can still hear the train if you listen."

Niya pressed her hands to her face, hiding her eyes. "No! I don't wanna listen! I don't wanna see any more!"

Remi gathered her to him again, seeing a night scene outside the window so different from what the sunlight would show. Taking her hand, he whispered, "Maybe we should go into the living room. It is now past three-thirty. We can wait there for the train to return and then this thing will be over."

But Niya stiffened, sitting up straight once more. She wiped tears from her face with savage swipes of her hands. "No! It'll only be over for *tonight!*" Her eyes grew fearful, staring around the shadowy room. "Remi? It ain't never gonna stop, is it? It ain't never gonna go away!" Then her eyes began to harden. "Remi, there's got to be a reason we saw this!"

He pressed her hand, saying gently, "The reason may only be that we are *here* to see it, Niya, that we somehow tuned into it ourselves. You are trying to use the logic of the living to explain what is not, or what is *no longer*, alive."

"No! You said we prob'ly couldn't change nuthin'. But we can move! We ain't stuck at the window like you were!" Niya suddenly leaped from the bed. "Remi! C'mon!"

For a second he stared as she bolted for the door, then he followed—out into the hall, down the dark stairs at a stumbling run. . . . He caught her before she could unlock the back door, slamming his palm against it.

"Niya, no! Wait! *Think!* What if *he* is out there now?"

Niya's eyes looked wild in the slim shaft of moonlight sifting through the door's curtained window. "My . . . my mom's got a gun!"

Remi grabbed the girl and shook her hard. "Yes! A gun! The American way to solve everything! Are you going to cap the ass of a ghost?"

Niya quieted, then finally nodded. "I guess you were right, what you said. Nuthin' here seems to make any sense."

"The sense it is making is only to itself, Niya. It is like a . . . player . . . in its own club, and we are outsiders here."

"But we're not *here*, Remi. Or *there*. Or wherever it is . . . Look!" Niya pointed to the black plastic garbage can by the door, something that could not have existed in 1943. "So we're still *here*, an' not there. Right?"

"I wish I knew more." Remi let go of Niya's shoulders and stepped to the door, hesitating with his hand on the knob. "Maybe there is no harm in trying to look. And maybe we will see nothing more than what will be out there when the sun comes up."

Niya pulled back the bolts. "Only one way to find out."

Remi took her hand again. "Yes. But *carefully*, Niya!"

He drew the door open, staying inside and peering cautiously around the frame while Niya looked over his shoulder. He sucked a startled breath. Beyond the small porch the house's back-yard had changed. The grass was weedy and still needed cutting, but the yard was no longer an untended jungle. The moonlight was bright and he scanned the scene quickly: no lawn chairs, no tire, and the toolshed stood whole. He heard Niya gasp, but then she tried to push past him. He tensed and gripped her hand tighter, flicking his eyes to the garbage can. It was still there, but it was *inside* the house. What would happen to that present-day thing if it was put outside? He drew back from the door-way, not even daring to slip the toe of his Nike over the threshold.

"Listen!" he whispered.

In the distance, beyond the back fence where the shipyard's arc-lamps glared, could be heard the slow rhythmic panting of a steam locomotive at rest. There was a squealing and clanking of big cranes swinging their booms and crawling around on their treads. But closer, out on the tracks and walking away, came the crunching of gravel beneath heavy boots.

"He's gettin' away!" hissed Niya. "C'mon!"

Before Remi could stop her, Niya shoved past him and ran down the steps into the yard. Without thinking, he followed. Then they both stopped and stood, suddenly unsure. Just as he had up in Mrs. Marcus's apartment, Remi felt the sensation of having stepped back in time—strange and yet somehow familiar. The house rose behind them in the silver moonlight, pale under paint just a few years from new, yet Remi could still see the garbage can inside the back door.

Niya noticed it, too. "I guess that means we can still go back, huh?"

Remi let out a sigh. "It would have been wise to check out that fact *before* running like fools into this place! Damn it, we do not know the laws here! Our parents have not now been born, and yet we exist! *Carefully*, Niya!"

Niya nodded, but then turned and pointed. "Remi! The basement doors! They ain't boarded up no more! An' I can smell fresh-dug dirt!"

Remi could, too. He noted with a chill that the toolshed door stood open, and thought of the faded old picture of Randy Marcus with a shovel in his hand. He turned back to the house. Like the yard itself, the flower beds had been left to run wild. Bushes and plants, their names unknown to him, had grown thick and tall. At the track-side corner of the house was the tangle of blackberry vines that would take over the place in the coming years. They were formidable now, but mostly confined to the fence like a brambly shroud. It was no surprise to see that the gate in the fence stood open, revealing the glimmer of moonlight on rails beyond. Remi looked to the basement doors: they were shut but, as Niya had said, unboarded. Could she have been right after all? *Had* the murderer buried the black man's body down there? Feeling a shiver, he took a step toward the doors, but now it was Niya who grabbed his hand.

"No! He's dead! I don't wanna go down there! You were right, Remi, this *happened*. An' nuthin' we tried to do stopped it from happenin'. But there's gotta be a reason for us bein' here now. C'mon!"

Reluctantly, his mind a whirl of confusion, Remi let himself be towed by Niya at a trot through the gate. The track looked recently laid, the rails just lightly rusted and gleaming silver where the train wheels had run. The gravel was sharp and sparkly-gray, and the ties smelled strongly of creosote. A few leftover spikes and rail-bed plates lay scattered about. Niya led Remi onto the tracks, then paused, looking toward the shipyard, shading her eyes against the blazing lights. There in the distance a huge hull was forming.

Despite his uncertainty, Remi felt awe. "It said in the books that a whole ship was built here and launched in a *week!*"

"It also said that *we* done most of the work!" Niya turned to Remi. "There's one of 'em left—

today, what I sayin'. It's in the bay, sorta like a museum. Maybe you an' me can go see it sometime?"

"We may be seeing it *now!*"

Niya peered toward the shipyard again. "There he goes! C'mon!"

"But . . ."

"Yo! We *are* players here, Remi! An' this ain't no stupid-ass G game! This *matters!* C'mon!"

Together, they started to trot up the tracks. Passing the switch, Remi caught a faint scent of sulphur. There on a tie lay a burned wooden match where the man had paused to light his cigarette. They broke into a run, nearing the shipyard now. It was surrounded by a tall chain-link fence topped by strands of barbed wire. There were gates standing open where the rails passed through. Not far inside stood the train. Its red tail lamp seemed like a warning to stop and go back. Ahead of the long line of flatcars, smoke spiraled from the locomotive's stack. Streamers of steam swirled from its sides as it panted at rest. Everywhere was urgent activity beneath glaring lights on tall wooden poles. A dozen big crawler cranes labored like eager dinosaurs to unload the train.

The shadows of workmen ran here and there as huge hooks swung and thick cables creaked. Heavy chains rattled, and trucks came and went with a rumble and roar, their headlights blazing like dragons' eyes through the haze of their own exhaust smoke. The train seemed to be half unloaded already. Remi watched, amazed. It was no wonder that ships had been built here so fast, and yet fifty years later everything would be silence and rust.

At the gate was a small watchman's shack. Light shone from its doorway, and there was the shape of a man at a desk. Remi and Niya came to a stop in the shadows outside the gates. Then, cautiously, they edged closer. The watchman seemed to be busy with paperwork. They dashed through the gates and crouched in the darkness behind what looked like a ship's boiler on huge timber skids. They peered around the side of the massive iron cylinder.

"I can't see him no more!" whispered Niya.

Remi scanned the area. "How can we hope to find him in all of this?"

"He can't have got far. We seen him come through the gates."

Remi shook his head. "We do not even know what he looks like, Niya. Most of these workmen are dressed the same way." He waved around at the endless activity under the glaring arc-lamps. "And we are only children here. We slipped past the watchman, but how far can we get without being noticed? What would we say to someone who stopped us? What if we were caught as trespassers? How could we live when we are not even born?"

Niya gave him a glance. "Yo! I thought you was s'posed to be down with 'manifestations,' Remi. You s'posed to know all that stuff." She gave him an uncertain look. "You sayin' you only been frontin'?"

"Fronting? . . . Oh. Well, not too much."

"Oh, *merde,* Remi!" She considered, then pointed around. Yo! All these people ain't nuthin' but ghosts, right? What I sayin' is, the train engineer didn't see us, the brutha didn't see us, an' we cruised past the watchman. Maybe *nobody* can see us here."

"Mmm. It is an interesting idea. In this place *we* may be the ghosts." Remi frowned and studied the train. "But even ghosts are bound to laws."

"Now what you sayin'? We gotta bring our own sheets or somethin'?"

"Listen, Niya, and do not make jokes. We are not just seeing ghosts. This is no simple haunting, and I feel that we are a *lot* farther from our home than a walk down those tracks. This manifestation is over when the train returns past my window. That is the end, and it could be ours, too, if we are not in my room when it passes away!"

Niya's eyes widened in the darkness. "You sayin' we could be stuck here?"

"Not 'here,' Niya. *Here* does not exist in the world of the living!" Remi gazed around. "I do not believe that these shapes we see are all ghosts—at least not like the man we followed. It cannot be that everyone dead becomes a *fantôme*. If that were so, then ghosts would outnumber the living a billion times over. It is also not likely that all of these men are dead in our own time."

He scanned around again. "I am sorry for 'fronting,' Niya, but my feelings tell me that all this is just a shadow play put on by the *fantôme* who brings the ghost train. He is a spirit still bound to this earth. What we see now can only be what *he* saw in his last living moments. When the ghost train is gone, there will be no more."

"What you sayin' is, no more till tomorrow night?"

"And who will be there to watch from the window if we are not?"

"Oh, *shit!*" Niya cast an uneasy glance back down the glimmering rails toward the house. "Then we don't got much time! The train's almost unloaded now! How fast does it go, backin' up?"

"No faster than a walk. I think we could easily outrun it. But we *must* be back in my room when it passes!"

Then Niya's finger stabbed out. "*Look!* There he is! He's goin' into that car on the back of the train."

Yes. Remi saw the man. He had kept to the shadows of a long line of crated machinery and emerged at the edge of the arc-lamps. His movements were wary. He did not want to be seen. Yet his manner seemed to change as he mounted the steps on the rear of the caboose. Now he looked confident, safe. A dim yellow glow shone out for a moment as he opened a door and entered.

"Yo!" whispered Niya. "You figure he works on the *train*? Maybe he's the conductor."

Remi considered. "It could be. But probably not a conductor. This is only a shuttle train. I have seen them in Haiti. Likely it is made up here in the port and runs only to this shipyard each night. He is maybe . . . a *brakeman!*"

Niya touched his shoulder. "Why did you say it like that? Is it important?"

"It might be. Last night, when the train returned, there was a man on the caboose—to keep watch because the engine is so far behind. Niya, that could be him!"

"But wouldn't he be missed, if he's s'posed to be on the train?"

"From what I have seen of trains, a brakeman would only be needed for setting switches and to watch when the train backs up. Niya, if this is the same man who murdered the brother, then he would know his duties tonight—and he would *know* how much time he had to bury the body and get back to his train!"

"Yeah! He'd have a watch!" Niya peered at her

own, holding it close to her face in the dimness. "Damn! It ain't workin'! I just bought a new battery last week."

Remi looked, too. "Maybe it is that digital watches have not been invented yet, and so are unknown to this manifestation."

"But *we're* here." Niya checked the sleeve of her shirt. "An' our clothes are here." She pointed down. "Did they have Nikes and Cons in 1943?"

"There were similar clothes made of similar things." Remi smiled slightly and touched his bare chest. "And there were kids just like us. *Laws*, Niya. Ghosts are not gods, and never has a ghost revealed knowledge beyond its own life span."

"Oh . . ."

Remi scanned the train once more. "But time is still passing in this place, and it cannot be much longer until the train leaves. See, there are only a handful of flatcars left to be unloaded."

"But we can't let him get away! You just said there were laws here!" Niya stepped out from the boiler's shadow.

Remi grabbed the tail of her sweatshirt and pulled her back. "Not those kind of laws, Niya!

Do you mean to go find a *fantôme* policeman?" He pointed to the train. "In minutes he will be gone anyway—vanished—and we along with him if we do not get back soon."

Niya struggled to get loose. "Goddammit, then why are we here?"

"Niya! Understand! We have *already* caught him! Somewhere there are records of the men who ran this train in 1943."

Niya snorted. "Yo, Remi! Get a clue! I don't know what the laws are like where you come from, but this's America! Cops don't care about dead black people *today!* What you figure they gonna do 'bout some poor brutha gettin' his ass capped fifty years ago?"

"But what if the murderer is already dead in our time?"

Niya tore free but paused to face Remi. "You said it yourself, boy, this thing's its own game. But *I* got a feelin' we just might be players in it." She grabbed Remi's arm. "So, c'mon an' let's go bust us a ghost!"

Not caring now about being seen, Remi followed Niya as she ran toward the train. Suddenly, a truck swung around the corner of a stack of steel plates. Its headlights swept over them, blinding them. They were caught full in the beams, yet the oncoming truck didn't swerve or slow down. Remi shoved Niya to one side, then dove to the dirt on the other. He rolled clear and twisted around, looking up. The truck had an open cab. Its driver was casually puffing a cigarette. The vehicle rumbled away, trailing dust.

"Niya!" Remi scrambled to his feet, relief flooding him when he saw Niya doing the same.

"Stupid asshole!" Niya flipped a finger after the truck's fading taillight. "Is it just 'cause we're niggers an' they don't give a shit?"

Remi came over to her. The zipper had torn on his jacket and he brushed dust from his body. "The driver was a black man. I do not think he would have run us down. Maybe they truly cannot see us."

Niya considered that. " 'Cause, like you said, they ain't real ghosts?"

Remi frowned, gazing after the truck. "Maybe. But I am beginning to suspect this place is only 'real' to someone else's eyes."

"So, what you sayin' is, that truck really couldn't hurt us?"

"I would not want to find out. Come. Time is short."

They started to run once again, approaching the back of the train from the shadows as the man had done. The red lamp cast an eerie crimson glow over their faces and reflected from their eyes as they neared the caboose. They stopped at the rear platform steps, and Remi reached up to grasp the railing. The iron was icy to his touch, but solid and real. Together he and Niya mounted the platform and, stepping lightly, moved to the narrow door. There was a single small window, and dim yellow light shone out through its soot-covered glass. Cautiously, Remi looked inside, feeling the car shift on its springs as the workmen continued to unload the train. Niya crowded close behind, peering over his shoulder.

The interior of the car was lit by a kerosene lamp that hung from an overhead hook. There were unmade beds that looked like bunks on a ship built into the woodwork along the walls, and a ladder led up on each side to the cupola above. A cast-iron stove stood in the far corner, a coal bin beside it. The night was warm, yet small flames flickered behind the fire door's grille. A green enamel coffeepot sat on the stove top and a wisp of steam ghosted from its spout. Remi could smell the coffee, somehow comforting even across fifty years, and the glow of the lamp reminded him of places and times in his life he could never return to.

Across from the stove, next to what could have been a closet, was a small built-in desk. Above it were shelves and pigeonholes, some stuffed with papers and documents. More papers lay on the desktop, and a pair of heavy gloves had been thrown down, scattering dirt over the papers. A chair was drawn up to the desk, but the man was nowhere in sight.

Remi pointed his fingertip to the grimy glass. He kept his voice to a whisper, even though the sounds of the shipyard rumbled and clashed and echoed all around. "There is another door at the other end. Maybe he has gone out to watch the work."

"Yo. What's that little room by the desk? You think it's a bathroom?"

"Mmm. Probably . . . on an American train. And water to wash with."

"Specially after diggin' a grave!" Niya drew back from the window. "Remi? You figure *he* could see us?"

"Again, Niya, I just do not know. But I feel there is something wrong here. There is a difference between this man and the others—the engineer and the truck driver. It may be because they were not part of the murder."

"So, like you said, they ain't real ghosts?"

"In a way they are like . . . someone else's *memories*."

"So, what you figure a *real* ghost could do to us?"

Remi took Niya's hand and laid it on the platform's rail. "Feel. It is cold and hard. Hit it with your fist; it causes pain." He reached up to touch the glowing red lens of the lamp. "It is hot. There is a flame inside. I would not put a finger into it. The train *is* a part of this thing, and now both we and the *fantôme* are on it!"

Niya nodded slowly, then turned again toward the door. Suddenly she gasped and shrank back against the railing. "Remi!" she whispered. "There he is!"

Remi kept Niya away from the door and the sooty window. Inside, the man had stepped out of the washroom and was drying his hands on a towel. He was still dressed in denim, as Remi had first seen him. The knees of his trousers were darkened with dirt. He looked to be in his mid-twenties, though his face was already hard—not so much cruel as uncaring and cold. Remi had seen many such faces on policemen and soldiers, on shopkeepers, clerks, and immigration officials. He had seen those same faces already on American TV. Not all were white, but all seemed to harbor some secret hate. The man wore a greasy blue railroad cap, and the hair beneath was the color of straw. A day's growth of beard about the same shade showed on his jawline and chin. A scratch crossed his cheek, not deep but new. His skin was pale, as if seldom in the sun, and his eyes as he glanced toward the door had an icy blue edge like the engine's headlamp. They were eyes that went with the face, eyes that could search with suspicion but would never question in simple curiosity. He was tall, and looked thin in his loose-fitting clothes, suggesting a rawboned body whose strength lay in sinew, not muscle. He seemed like a man who would endure life but never really live it.

Remi felt a rising anger within him. Fifty years would not punish a man such as this. Where was he now? Retired with a pension? Still in this city? If so, did he sometimes come walking along the rusty old rails to gaze at the house and remember? Did he remember and *smile*?

And then Remi had a moment of doubt. He was not God, and had little right to be a judge. Why had this man killed another human being? Could there have been a justification? But then the man turned to the desk and pulled a thick roll of bills from his pocket, along with a wristwatch and worn leather wallet. He lay them on the desktop, and his fingers moved fast, counting the money.

"Bastard!" hissed Niya.

All doubt vanished from Remi's mind as the man took a few more bills from the wallet, scanned through some papers inside, then opened the stove's fire door and tossed the wallet into the flames. Finally, he pulled a big railroad watch from another pocket and glanced at the time.

"Yes," Remi whispered, "there can be no justification for what he has done!"

From in front of the line of flatcars came two short hoots on the locomotive's whistle. The man swept the money and watch into his coat pocket, then reached for a lantern that hung from a hook near the desk. He opened the lantern's top, struck a match, and fired the wick. From his shirt pocket he pulled out a green-colored pack of Lucky Strikes, slipped one between his lips, and lit it with the same match.

Suddenly Niya shoved Remi aside and threw open the door. "You goddamn murderin' bastard!"

For a second Remi could only stare in amazement as Niya burst into the car. Almost distractedly he wondered what would happen now. He half expected nothing at all; that the man, like a shadow in an old movie, would only go on with his role. But instead the man screamed! He dropped the lantern, which hit the floor and went out. The cigarette fell from his lips, landing beside the lantern in a burst of bloody sparks. Then Remi realized that the man was staring *past* Niya, staring at *him*, his eyes wide in horror.

With another cry the man stumbled back, throwing his arm out for balance. His hand came down on the hot stove top. He screamed again, backing farther away to cower against the door at the front of the car. Niya had frozen but now she stepped toward the man, cursing him again. For an instant his eyes rolled up, showing white as if he would faint and fall to the floor. His burned hand, still smoking, clutched at the doorknob behind him, but all the while his eyes stayed locked in terror on Remi.

But then, slowly, a change began to come over his face. His eyes now narrowed and shifted, focusing a moment on Niya and then returning to Remi, as if he were a child who had found an unburied skull and was gathering courage to touch it. The terror started to fade from his face and suspicion crept in to replace it. At the same time, a new feeling began to take hold of Remi, a feeling he couldn't yet name.

Then a red glare of rage appeared in the icy blue eyes. The man swallowed, then straightened up, still keeping his back to the door. He realized pain; his mouth twisted as he clutched his burned hand in the other. Finally he found his voice, uncertain at first but sharpening to a brittle edge:

"W-what are you little niggers doing on this train? . . . Get off! I'll bust your god-damn heads!"

Remi took Niya's arm and drew her aside, stepping in front of her and facing the man. His jacket hung open, and he felt a cold like the chilling of steam on his body. No matter: now he would put a *fantôme* on its back! "Who were you?" he demanded.

A new flicker of fear crossed the man's face as he stared at Remi, but then his expression turned cunning. His hand must have been in agony, yet a sneer of disgust curled his lips.

"Don't you mean who *am* I, boy?"

Remi himself wasn't sure why he'd said that. Hardly a minute ago he'd been wondering where this man might be fifty years from now. But a coldness seemed to come from the figure before him, a dark, lonely coldness, like a cold that eternally cursed the light and warmth it hungered for. Remi could feel Niya's warmth beside him, and the heat from the stove against his chest, yet only cold seemed to come from the man. Then Remi realized why.

"No. Who *were* you? Because you are dead!"

Once more a shadow of fear seemed to cross the man's face. It was almost as if he was trying to remember some long-ago thing. But then, slowly, he let go of his burned hand and the other crept toward his coat pocket.

"You goddamn monkeys got no business on my train! I'm telling you one more time to get off! Get the *hell* off, or *you're* the one who's gonna be dead, nigger boy!"

Again came two short blasts of the locomotive's whistle. The man's eyes flicked to the lantern at Remi's feet. An awareness was growing in Remi, a realization that he had to stay in control, that the man must not be allowed to remember the past. He didn't know why this seemed so important, but something inside him warned that it was. He pointed to the man's coat pocket.

"No! You will not shoot us as you shot that man tonight! This train is now ready to leave! The engineer is waiting for your signal! You have no time to kill us and bury our bodies!"

Remi darted a glance at Niya. The fury had faded from her face and now she was calmly watching him, trusting him to know what to do, and he could only hope he was doing the right thing.

"Tell us your name. Then you may go."

Another blast of the whistle—a single one, longer and urgent.

Remi touched the lantern with his toe, seeing the man's eyes follow his move. Somehow this was like playing a game. The cold from the man seemed to be seeping into Remi's bones. No! It was really *two* games! A game within a game. To lose one was death, but losing both would trap them between death and the ghost train forever!

He had been a fool! His father's books were filled with warnings! The icy cold now clutched at his heart like skeleton fingers but he forced his voice to command:

"Carefully, *blanc*. You cannot risk having anyone suspect where you were tonight. You cannot have anyone question why you were not here to perform your duties. You must give the signal for this train to start, and soon, or you *will* be suspected. This must not happen because you were digging a grave when you should have been on your train!" Remi forced a smile. "Hear that?

The engine men are already wondering where you are."

The man's eyes went suddenly wild, glazing with hate like an animal trapped. "You . . . god-dammed *nigger!*" He lunged for Remi.

"Niya! Run!"

Niya spun around and dashed through the door. Remi dodged, but the man caught hold of his sleeve. Twisting desperately, Remi slipped out of the jacket, wincing as the man's fingers, impossibly cold, clutched his bare shoulder. He tore free and ran out onto the platform, and together he and Niya leaped to the ground as the man burst from the doorway behind them, the gun in his hand.

Around the train all was quiet. A few shadows of men moved away toward the lights. One of the big cranes idled at rest and two others clanked slowly away on their treads. The trucks had all been driven off with their loads to other parts of the shipyard. Would the man risk a shot? Remi wondered. He and Niya had stopped a few paces down the track. They now stood, ready to run but watching the man. Remi touched his shoulder, still numbed by the man's icy fingers. Could a bullet reach them across fifty years?

The man seemed ready to fire, sighting on Remi at the edge of the light, a small black target against deeper darkness. But then the locomotive blew a long angry blast, and cursing, the man dashed back inside.

Spinning around, Remi grabbed Niya's hand. "Run! We must beat the train home!"

They raced down the tracks, their shoes pounding the gravel and ties. Her braids streaming behind her, Niya panted, "But we didn't do nuthin'! We didn't change nuthin'!"

"No!" he panted back. "We changed *everything!* Run!"

Ahead were the gates. Remi saw the watchman leaning in the doorway, his cigarette a crimson spark. He was looking toward the train, and so also at them, yet he seemed not to see them at all. Keeping hold of her hand, Remi pulled Niya on past the shack. They might have been less than ghosts to the watchman, no more than a whisper of breeze in the night. He didn't turn his eyes from the train. Through the open doorway Remi caught sight of a clock on the wall. Its hands stood at 4:45. Eight minutes left to get back to his room.

Niya tried to slow down, dragging on Remi's hand. "You said the train don't come very fast. We'll make it, Remi. Easy!"

Remi shot a look over his shoulder. The man was now frantically signaling the locomotive with his lantern. There was a long whistle blast, then three shorter ones. Air spat from under the cars as the brakes were released. The slow and ponderous puffing of steam throbbed through the night. Steel wheels shifted and creaked, starting to roll. Remi kept hold of Niya's hand, pulling her along.

"I was a fool! Our only hope is that he will not believe what a nigger boy told him! He still thinks he is on the train!"

"I don't understand."

"Just . . . believe in the train, Niya! We have made it late! It *cannot* be late! It will come faster! *Run!*"

New fear showed in Niya's eyes, yet she was strong. Her face grew determined and she picked up speed. Gravel skittered and flew from their shoes as they raced down the track. The train whistle screamed like something in rage, and the chuffing of steam grew louder. The empty cars rattled and creaked, and their couplings clattered and clashed. The clanking and clang of their wheels came echoing down the rails.

Ahead was the house, pale in the moonlight. There was the fence with its curtain of brambles, and there was the gate standing open. There was the switch and beyond it escape, but behind came the train ever faster!

It took concentration to run on the tracks, not to slip in the gravel or trip on a tie. There was no time left to get up from a fall, yet Remi risked a look behind.

The man stood on the platform. His face seemed bathed in blood by the lamp. His grin was crimson and ghastly, and the gun seemed to glow red-hot in his hand. A flash of fire spat from the muzzle. The sound of the shot was lost in the rumble and clash of the train. The bullet twanged off a rail near Remi's foot. There was nowhere to run but straight down the tracks, no *time* to dodge aside. Niya threw a glance over her shoulder. Her eyes reflected the lamp's scarlet glare. She was slowing, tiring, she tripped and almost fell. Remi's own breath burned in his throat. He managed to gasp:

"It is . . . good that he shoots! . . . Faster, Niya!"

"*Good?* . . . Does he . . . know . . . we got to . . . get back to the house?"

"Pray God he does not!" Remi let go of Niya's hand, urging her on with a push. "RUN!"

Behind came the train. Remi could hear it gaining on them. The shriek of its whistle rang in his ears. But there just ahead was the switch. Niya was now a few paces in front of him. Then she was passing the switch. Remi started to believe they *would* make it home! For all of its power, its great pounding pistons, its roaring of fire and spewing of steam, the train could not catch them!

And then Niya fell! She screamed, twisting around and clutching her ankle, caught in the **Y** of the switch. Remi skidded to a stop. Niya screamed again as he grabbed her foot and dragged her backward, free of the rails.

"Niya! Get up! Run!"

Sobbing, her tears like blood in the hideous

light, she tried to get to her feet. "I . . . *can't!*"

The train rocked and rumbled toward them, the man on the platform grinning, aiming his gun. Desperately, Remi pulled Niya up and tried to get her off the tracks. He looked back. The gun seemed aimed at his heart. In seconds the train would be on them.

Then he let Niya fall. She screamed his name but he ran, back up the tracks toward the oncoming train.

"REMI!"

Stumbling, almost falling, he reached the switch. A frantic second was wasted while he figured out how to work it. Then he yanked the handle free of its latch and struggled to swing it around. The mechanism was almost new, yet needed the strength of a man to move it. Remi threw all his weight on the handle, fighting to shift it, his back in an arch, teeth bared in a snarl, his shoes skidding and kicking the gravel. The rails moved, but only a little. Again he struggled and wrenched at the handle. Little by little it gave. An inch at a time, the heavy rails shifted, but slowly . . . too slowly.

On came the train. The man's face was twisted in rage. The gun bucked in his hands, firing twice. A bullet hissed past Remi's ear. Another ricocheted off the switch post. Then a third sprayed gravel and a chip ripped across Remi's cheek. Still he struggled to shift the rails. The handle was halfway around. Would there be time?

And then Niya was beside him. Her hands grasped the iron over his own. She fought along with him to drag the handle around. Another shot. Niya cried out and fell, but the rails had been shifted.

Remi grabbed Niya under the arms and pulled her away down the track. There was nowhere to go and no time to do anything else. From behind came the man's roar of rage. Remi turned, tensing in horror as the man leaped from the platform. Remi stood, sheltering Niya, as the man hit the ground at a run and raced toward them. But then the man stumbled, his foot slipping on one of the leftover track plates. He fell. A scream tore from his throat, echoing over the shriek of the whistle and pounding of wheels as the train ran him down.

There was no time left for anything. Remi gathered Niya against him, staring into a hellish red eye that seemed to bathe the whole world in blood. But then came a screeching and grinding and squealing of steel as the train lurched onto the other track. The red light vanished. The line of cars passed, rocking and clanking. At last came the engine. Steam gushed in a cloud over Remi, an instant of searing hot pain on his body, and then it was gone. The last thing he saw was the icy blue shaft of the headlamp, leaving him blind as it slowly faded away into an unguessable distance, until there was nothing at all.

Nothing.

Only the darkness and silence that could have been death.

And yet . . .

Gradually, through ears still numbed from the thunder of the train, Remi began to hear other sounds: a distant siren, the rumble of trucks on a highway . . . someone sobbing.

"Niya! Are you all right?"

Tears glistened on her cheeks. She struggled to sit up, and her voice held almost more wonder than pain. "I . . . think I got shot. Goddammit, I *did!*" She clutched at her side.

Remi pulled up her sweatshirt, dripping wet like his body from steam. Blood was warm on his fingers, glistening black in the moonlight. He bent close, but then sighed in relief.

"It does not seem deep. A gash. The bullet did not go in."

But she stared around now in new fear. "Remi! We didn't make it home!"

He looked around. They were still on the tracks. Then he let out a longer sigh. The rails were rotted with rust. Weeds grew tall between them. He looked to the house: moonlight was kind, but the paint was peeling in places and the fence was half fallen and buried by blackberry brambles. A light shone pale and lonely in the gabled window on the topmost floor. He held Niya close, savoring her warmth. "We are home."

"But . . . we wasn't at your window when the train came back."

Remi glanced at the ghost track that led toward the bay. "It never returned past our house that night."

"Huh? What you sayin'?"

Remi smiled. "Because we sent it away."

"Whoa!"

"Can you walk? I will help you. Um, will your mother have a cow?"

"Prob'ly. But she always did say I'd get my fool self shot someday."

Niya bit her lip as Remi helped her to her feet. He drew her arm over his shoulder, but she tensed and pointed toward the switch. "Remi! What's *that?*"

Remi looked where she pointed, a little ways past the rusted switch post. "I will go check it out."

"Take me with you."

Leaning on Remi, Niya limped beside him up the track. Then they both stopped and stared. A skeleton lay half-crushed on the rails. There were only rotted remnants of clothing, tatters and shreds of what might have been denim. Many seasons of weeds had grown up through the bones. The skull faced them, its jaws gaping wide, eternally screaming. Grass grew in the empty eye sockets. Near one bony claw lay a rusted revolver. Niya took Remi's hand and they stood for a time looking down at the silent white thing. Then Niya asked:

"Remi? Back there . . . what I sayin' is, back *there* . . . when we was runnin' from the train, why did you say you was a fool?"

Remi sighed. "Well, you see, in all of my father's books that deal with the supernatural there is, how you say, rule number one. Never, never, *never* tell a ghost he is dead."

Niya cocked her head. "Why?"

"Well, it tends to . . . piss them off."

"Mmm. Got that right! But how much power did he have over us?"

Remi looked down at the long bony fingers that had clutched his shoulder only minutes before. He shivered. "Far more than he dreamed."

"What you sayin'? An' why you keep talkin' 'bout dreams?"

Remi touched the small wooden cross on its leather strip. "*Voodun* teaches that the spirit within each of us is the thinker of our thoughts, and my father has suggested that a haunting may be the dream of the haunter." He pointed to the bones. "When we were . . . *there*, we existed as *fantômes* in a place that was mostly his dream. And in my own fronting foolishness I almost woke the sleeper."

Niya thought for a moment. "But wouldn't that have capped it?"

Remi gazed down the grass-grown ghost track once more. "But where do dreams go when the sleeper wakes? My jacket is still on the train!" He shook his head. "My mother will have a cow."

Niya's eyes had gone wide. "Whoa!" She stared at the skeleton again. "But what you sayin', it was *mostly* his dream?"

"I do not think he would have wanted us in it, chasing and accusing him for all eternity."

"Sounds like we turned his dream into a nightmare."

Remi smiled. "Yes. But we could not have done it alone. Someone gave us the power to enter and change it."

Niya snapped her fingers. "Yeah! It was the brutha! So he *is* buried down in our basement!"

Remi had turned back to study the yard—the half-collapsed toolshed, the jungle of blackberry vines. "No. He is not buried in the basement."

"Huh? Now what you sayin', Remi?"

Remi just fingered his jaw. "I will need a certain tool. My mother has told me of a flea market that sells such things. Can you tell me how to get there?"

Niya regarded him for a moment. "I'll take you."

"But you are hurt."

Niya pulled up her sweatshirt once more. Both examined the gash on her side. In the growing light of dawn it didn't look serious: the bleeding had stopped and the blood was drying, beginning to flake from her skin.

"Hell," she said. "I got hurt worse in a fight in girls' P.E."

"But your ankle?"

"I'll soak it in cold water awhile." Then Niya frowned. "Yo! What's up, Remi? If the body ain't in the basement, then *where* is it?"

Remi sighed. "Come. We will see to your ankle and then I will tell you." He drew Niya's arm over his shoulder once more, but paused to look back at the switch. Long rusted solid, the rails were eternally set to send trains away from the house.

10

So, what you sayin' is, there never was no Tom Mix?"

Remi slashed at the last thorny vine with the glittering blade, then stood for a moment panting. He wore just his shoes and his shorts, and his ebony body gleamed in the sun-light. Niya had been dragging the brambles away down the trail he had cut. She wore heavy work gloves, but her arms and legs, bare in loose tank top and old cut-off jeans, were covered with scratches. She limped slightly, and her own dark chocolate skin glistened with sweat.

The rotten old boards of the fence were cleared of vines at the house's back corner. Below, the dirt was dark and damp. Niya's eyes shied from the ominous shape where the ground had sunk.

Remi scanned the earth for a moment. There didn't seem to be any urgency now to uncover what must lay below. The police would have to be called, and he didn't care for that thought, though he almost smiled picturing their reaction to what lay out on those time-rusted rails. He lifted the machete and sighted along it for trueness, but really to put off a moment or two the task they had to complete.

"The blade seller at the flea market had many old pocketknives that were treasured by yesterday's children and engraved with the names of their heroes—Buck Rogers, Flash Gordon . . . and Tom Mix, a Saturday movie cowboy. No wonder Mrs. Marcus looked at me strangely when I asked about him."

Niya smiled. "Cowboys an' spacemen. None of 'em were real, an' none of 'em were black, but they still musta given kids of all colors good things to dream about."

Remi nodded. "I wonder who are the heroes of American children today?" He pulled the knife from his pocket. "Still, I may always think of the boy in my room as Tom Mix. It seems a much braver name than Iceman or Monster or something else 'G'." He offered the knife. "Would you like it, Niya?"

She took it and smiled again. "*Merci*, Remi. I

got a feelin', whoever he was, Tom was a lot like you."

"*Merci*, Niya." Then Remi gazed down at the ground. "I suppose we must do this thing now."

Niya reached for the old shovel but then hesitated. "Remi? Do we really got to? What I sayin' is, it's been fifty years, and the murderer's dead. Does it even matter anymore?"

Remi opened a palm toward the earth. "It matters to him."

Niya looked troubled. "What do you think *really* happened to the *blanc*?"

"What really happened *has* happened. He was run down by his train . . . over fifty years ago."

"Chasing *us*?"

"That is what happened."

Niya shook her head. "I guess you was right, these things make a sense of their own." She glanced at her watch. "Just like this thing. It's keepin' *some* kinda time, but only between three-thirteen an' four fifty-three!"

"My father has said that encounters with the supernatural always change things in some way, so if they change people, why not watches?" Remi smiled. "So maybe you, too, now have an affinity for spirits . . . and they for you."

Niya considered that for a moment, then shrugged. "Ain't much I can do about it now, is there?" She looked down again. "So, how did you figure the brutha was buried out here?"

Remi leaned on the machete once more. "Last night, remember that we both smelled freshly dug dirt?" He smiled again. "In your eagerness to bust a ghost you gave me no time to think about what that might mean. It was only after our escape from the train that I began to wonder. As we found yesterday, there was nothing buried in the basement—"

"But," broke in Niya, "what about the feelin's? An' the shadow, or whatever it was we both saw?"

"Yes. But remember that those feelings came from the corner, and that the shadow seemed to come *out* of the wall instead of, as the saying goes, 'rising from the grave.' And no wonder, when the grave is here, outside. Did you see on the desk in the caboose a pair of gloves covered with dirt? Mrs. Marcus advised me to buy such gloves because of these thorns. Remember, too, the *blanc* had a scratch on his cheek? After I had time to think all this over, it seemed only logical that the *blanc* had pushed aside this curtain of brambles and dug a shallow grave with the shovel from the toolshed. The ground was soft, time was short, why risk the basement?" He paused. "The strange thing is why he even buried the body at all. It seems that his only real concern would be to get it away from the tracks so it wouldn't be seen by the engine crew when the train passed the house again. I am still curious about that, but no matter. The yard as we saw was already neglected in 1943. Mrs. Marcus had lost her husband and had the house to run by herself. And her son, Randy, was not fond of dirt. Then he, too, was gone—away to sea, as his mother believes. So, nothing has been touched since that night long ago."

Niya glanced again at the ground, then stepped forward with the shovel. "I'll do it. You been swingin' that thing all mornin'."

It didn't take long. The earth was soft and the grave was shallow. Niya gasped and drew back at the first sight of bone, but then set her jaw and looked determined, laying down the shovel and kneeling beside Remi to dig with her hands as he did. Their fingers moved almost reverently among the same bones they had feared the day before. But now there was only a feeling of peace. Most of the clothing had long since been taken by the earth. There were a few shreds of denim and a scrap of leather belt with a square brass buckle corroded and green. Then Remi frowned as more was uncovered. Around the skeleton's neck was a slim chain and a pair of government ID tags. Made of stainless steel, they were tarnished but intact. Remi brushed away the clinging dirt, his eyes going wide as he read:

"Jeffery Marcus!"

Niya stared. "But . . . how did he get *here*? Mrs. Marcus said he was killed in the war."

Remi rocked back on his heels and thought for a time. "Mmm. No, not killed, 'presumed lost.' " He gazed down at the bones in silence awhile, then murmured, "Maybe it was as Mrs. Marcus dreamed—his own ship was sunk, but he was rescued by another. A foreign ship that took him far away. There was a war going on all over the world, and he was only a merchant sailor. And a black man. But somehow he made his way back to his wife and son. Another ship to the port here in Oakland . . ."

Remi glanced toward the tracks. "And there was a train. A night train going right past his house. Maybe he told the brakeman his story to get a ride. There was money to tempt the *blanc*, money belonging to a black man who was already thought to be dead."

Remi sighed. "So it *was* as she dreamed. Jeffery Marcus came home."

Niya looked up toward the gabled window. "Fifty years an' she never knew what really happened to him. It's sad. But at least she won't have to wonder no more."

"Yes. It seems we have solved this thing, but I still feel as if we are not yet finished."

Niya started to get up but then tensed and pointed at the grave. "Remi! Look!"

Remi stared for a second, then began digging again. Niya quickly joined him. "Remi! There's *another* skeleton!"

A new sense of peace came over Remi as they dug. There were more shreds of clothing, what looked to be dungaree jeans, and a small tennis shoe. "Stop," he told Niya. "We have done what we were called for." He shook his head. "At least, as you say, Mrs. Marcus will not spend the rest of her life never knowing what happened to them."

Remi crouched at the grave, gazing down, tears filling his eyes and falling among the small, fine bones.

"He was brave, as his mother said, brave to have run out here alone that night. And he died for his courage, facing his father's murderer." Remi wiped his eyes. "I should have remembered: she told me how happy he was to have his own room. But the ground floor was rented, and there is only *one* bedroom on the third."

Niya turned to him in wonder. Remi nodded. "He is Randy Marcus. And he is also Tom Mix, the boy who watched from my window."